There I Find Peace

Strawberry Sands Book Two

Jessie Gussman

Published By: Jessie Gussman

This is a work of fiction. Similarities to real people, places, or events are entirely coincidental. Copyright © 2023 by Jessie Gussman.

Written by Jessie Gussman.

All rights reserved.

No portion of this book may be reproduced in any form without written permission from the publisher or author, except as permitted by U.S. copyright law.

Contents

Acknowledgements   VI

1. Chapter 1   1

2. Chapter 2   24

3. Chapter 3   47

4. Chapter 4   66

5. Chapter 5   92

6. Chapter 6   117

7. Chapter 7   149

8. Chapter 8   168

9. Chapter 9   185

10. Chapter 10   208

11. Chapter 11   232

12. Chapter 12   268

13. Chapter 13   302

14. Chapter 14   318

15. Chapter 15   349

16. Chapter 16   362

17. Chapter 17   395

18. Chapter 18   418

19. Chapter 19   442

20. Chapter 20   452

21. Chapter 21   473

22. Chapter 22   494

23. Chapter 23   514

Epilogue   538

There I Find Love 552

A Gift from Jessie 569

Acknowledgements

Cover art by Kim Killion of The Killion Group

Editing by Heather Hayden

Narration by Jay Dyess

Author Services by CE Author Assistant

Listen to the unabridged audio for FREE performed by Jay Dyess on the Say with Jay channel on YouTube. Get early access to all of Jay's recordings and listen to Jessie's books before they're available to the general public, plus get daily Bible readings by Jay and bonus scenes by becoming a Say with Jay channel member .

<h1 style="text-align:center">Chapter 1</h1>

J ubilee's car sputtered.

You have got to be kidding me.

She didn't open her mouth because her two daughters, Scarlett and Penelope, sat in the back seat. They'd been driving for twelve hours, and they were both exhausted.

Her car sputtered again, and her fingers tightened on the steering wheel.

Please, Lord. Just ten more miles.

She glanced at the gas gauge, which showed it to have about a sixteenth of a tank, just slightly above the bottom Empty line.

That was one sixteenth, wasn't it?

Maybe that was wishful thinking.

"Mom, is the car going to break down?" Scarlett said from her position behind Jubilee's seat.

"I hope not," Jubilee gave her the honest answer.

"I hope it does. I'm sick of sitting in here." Penelope, eight, never hesitated to speak her mind.

She wanted to tell Penelope to keep her hopes to herself, because if their car broke down, it was going to be a very long time before Jubilee's day was over, and considering that twelve hours of driving would wear out anyone, she was ready for the day to be over. Ready for the week to be over. Ready for her life... She didn't want to think that, so she pulled those words back into her brain.

Truly, she didn't think things could get any worse. She wondered how long she was going to be living at the bottom, where things couldn't get any worse.

The car sputtered one more time, then the engine died.

All right, so when the gas gauge was just a little bit above the line, it didn't mean that there was one sixteenth of a gallon tank left. It meant that the little arrow couldn't go any lower.

At least the highway was wide and flat, unlike some of the hills that they'd been driving in earlier that day as they left Pennsylvania.

Those roads had a tendency to be winding and narrow, with high bridges that took her breath away and made her want to close her eyes.

Michigan was much different. Especially here along the lake. Strawberry Sands was just ten miles or so away, and it was right on the shore of Lake Michigan.

Lord, I was hoping we would make it. I thought You were going to help us get there. Wasn't that the deal? I would put everything I had into it, if You would just get us to Strawberry Sands.

She hadn't been sure at the time if God was really making that deal with her, or if she just really wanted the change of pace herself.

Strawberry Sands was one of the few happy memories she had from her childhood, a place of peace and comfort. A place where neighbors cared about each other and where it was safe to walk the streets. A place she'd like to raise her girls. Now that she finally left her cheating husband.

There was no point in thinking about that now. Currently, she had a problem sitting in front of her that she was going to have to solve before she got to go to bed tonight. If she even got to go to bed. After all, she wouldn't have run out of gas if she'd had the money to fill up her tank back in Blueberry Beach, when they passed the last gas station.

She'd been hoping to get to Strawberry Sands, hoping to get a job. Hoping to... She didn't know. She really didn't have plans for tonight, which probably showed what a terrible parent she actually was. But in a place like Strawberry Sands, they could sleep in their car, they could sleep along the beach, either place would be just as safe as sleeping in a two-story house with a white picket fence in the middle of small-town USA.

Still, normal adults didn't plan to house their children in their car for any length of time, even just one night.

Maybe she would have been better off staying with her husband.

Or, at the very least, staying with her mother-in-law. Which was where she moved when she found out that her husband had been cheating.

Not a smart move, since two nights ago, her mother-in-law had invited her husband and his new girlfriend over for dinner. She had expected Jubilee to have the girls at the table and to be welcoming to their "guest."

Jubilee knew that as a Christian, she needed to be kind, but as a human, her heart just hurt too hard for her to do much more than sit at the table and try not to cry.

She got up to get the dessert, and instead of getting it and taking it back in to the table, she slipped up the back stairs, going to her room and doing that very thing.

Hopefully God would understand. Actually, she knew He did. Jesus went through a trial at his crucifixion that had to have been just as painful. The Bible didn't record him crying, but that didn't mean he didn't.

After living through what she had, Jubilee suspected he had.

She fingered her cell phone as she sat along the road.

"Mom? What are you going to do?" Scarlett asked, and her voice didn't sound sweet and nice. It sounded rather demanding, like she expected her mother to fix this problem and now.

"You need to call a tow truck. He needs to have someplace to haul all of us to. Make sure of that when you call them." Penelope had to put her two cents in too. She acted older than an eight-year-old, probably because she was so smart. Jubilee wasn't sure where she got her intelligence, since it certainly wasn't from her. She was about the dumbest person in the world, and anyone who doubted it could just look at the decisions she made over the course of her life, if they needed to be convinced.

This latest decision, the one that made her just jump in her car and take off, was a case in point. Although, where she ended up started out with her decision to not open a new bank account only in her name.

She had had almost a thousand dollars, which wasn't a whole lot, but it was everything that she'd saved since she left her husband. She'd had to pay the lawyer's fees since her husband filed for divorce. And that had set her back, or she would have had more. Still, it had been a shock at noon when her card had been declined when she tried to buy lunch at a fast-food place along the interstate.

After doing some research, she realized that her husband had taken everything but ten bucks from the account.

She assumed it was him, since no one else had access to it. She had thought it was fraud and considered reporting it, but she would have felt like an idiot if the bank had said that it was her husband who took it. Still, she called, just to confirm. The lady at the bank had been super helpful. After all, she'd known Jubilee for years, since that's where they'd banked since they got married.

The lady had cheerfully informed Jubilee that her husband had, indeed, taken the money.

It was not coming back. And Jubilee knew there was nothing she could do about it. She wasn't the kind of person to beat a dead horse.

If she were, she might take this opportunity to cry. But of course, crying didn't solve anyone's problems, and she really didn't have time for that right now anyway. Actually, she did have time.

"I'm hungry," Scarlett whined from the back seat.

Okay. Maybe she didn't have a lot of time.

She sighed and tried to think of whether or not there was still a small package of peanuts in her purse. She couldn't even remember where she got it, but she did remember digging around them more than once, thinking that she should just take them out, and then reminding herself that someday she might want them.

She reached over the console and picked up her purse which sat on the passenger side.

Her wallet was in there of course, but it was empty.

After digging for a bit, she found the package of peanuts.

"This is all I have. It should tide you over until we figure things out."

She should call a tow, but she didn't have the money to pay. She didn't even have a credit card because when she left her husband, she'd cut them all up, knowing she couldn't afford to rack up a bunch of debt.

Buying things she didn't need wasn't ex-actly something she did a lot of, but she didn't want to be tempted. Tempted to buy things for her children to try to diminish the pain of not having a father living with them anymore.

Back when she was a young mother, back when she had stars in her eyes and dreams of being the best mom anyone had ever had, she'd determined in her heart that she would be a happy mom. Someone who made everything fun. Someone whom her children remembered as smiling every day and laughing freely.

Of course there were times when a person had to be serious, but she didn't want her children to remember her as someone who never laughed, or smiled, or had fun.

She wanted them to remember their childhood as joyful and happy.

She almost laughed. How could a child remember their childhood as joyful and happy when their parents split right in the middle of it, breaking up their home and tearing up everything that they thought was dependable and safe?

Still, her goal of being happy and joyful was still attainable, just harder.

For the most part, she felt like she'd done pretty well, but...it was always an effort. Especially at times like these when she really didn't know what to do, and she was scared and sad and alone.

"All right, girls, we're going to get to walk a little bit. The lake breeze always feels fresh and clean, and the first person who sees Lake Michigan gets a star."

"Mom. We're too old for the star thing," Scarlett said, and if a voice could roll its eyes, hers was rolling all over the place.

"All right. That's fine. If you don't want a star, I can give one to myself. Because I'm pretty sure I'm going to see the lake first," she said easily, opening up her door and stepping out. Her purse was the only thing of any value that she would want to take with her, but they probably should take a change of clothes as well.

Walking back to the trunk, she popped the hood and pulled her suitcase around so she could open it.

"Could someone just pick us up and give us a ride?" Scarlett said.

"Why aren't you calling a tow truck, Mom?" Penelope asked as her girls came around the back of the car.

She hadn't wanted them to worry about money. She hadn't wanted them to worry about anything. She wanted their childhoods to be safe and happy and secure. But what she wanted and what actually happened were obviously not going to be the same thing.

"I don't want to call a tow truck when I can't pay them for what they're going to do," she said matter-of-factly so that it didn't worry the girls. She had learned that it seemed like if she acted worried, then they became worried as well.

"So what are we gonna do?" Scarlett asked, probably understanding the implications of the fact that they couldn't afford to pay for a tow better than her younger sister. Even if her younger sister was the one who usually had something to say about it.

"We'll pray as we walk. We're going to be happy that we have legs. Happy that it's a beautiful summer day and not the middle of winter. It's cold up here in the winter. With lots of snow."

"I love snow!" Penelope said. "How soon is it going to snow?"

"Well, I'm not sure. I've never been here when it snows. But it's June, so probably not until fall." She looked back down at the suitcase. "I'm going to pull out an outfit for each of us that we can wear tomorrow, plus our night things."

The girls talked a bit as they chose an outfit to take, and Jubilee put them in a plastic grocery store bag.

They hadn't passed a single car for the last ten minutes they'd been driving, and no one had passed them since they had pulled over to the side of the road, so when she heard a motor floating over the quiet of the lake air, she picked her head up.

Should she try to stop them?

It turned out like so many things in her life she worried about—it resolved on its own.

When she straightened and turned around, the pickup coming toward her already had its turn signal on and was slowing down.

She supposed she probably should have been scared, but it made her smile. This was what Strawberry Sands was to her. People stopping to help other people, even if they were complete strangers. The townsfolk helped each other even more.

It was the kind of community she wanted to be a part of.

Still, she was expecting a kindly older gentleman, or maybe even a teenager, but the man who pulled up behind her and stepped out of his pickup was in his late twenties or early thirties, and handsome, as he shoved the cowboy hat down over his head and slammed his door closed. The stubble on his jaw was enough to make Jubilee's heart beat faster before she reminded her heart that handsome jaws and charming men made terrible husbands.

She would be the expert in that.

Her girls pushed closer to her side as the man walked toward them. His hand came out, and he lifted the brim of his hat just a little.

"I'm Matt. Looks like you might be needing some help."

Matt. She highly doubted it was the same Matt that she'd crushed on years ago, when she had spent the summer in Strawberry Sands. That was not why she was coming back. But she couldn't deny there was a part of her that longed for those sweet summer days when she sat on the beach and admired him as he rode his horse up and down the shore-line.

There were surfers in the water, boaters as well, but it was Matt and his horse that had always caught her eye.

"I'm Jubilee, and yeah. Unfortunately, I seem to have made bad decision after bad decision and am once more against the wall."

His face was serious, but one side of his mouth turned up, and her heart start-ed beating hard again. It didn't seem to listen to anything she said. That didn't mean she had to do whatever it wanted to. In fact, in her experience, she was better off if she did the exact opposite.

Chapter 2

Matt Landry stared at the woman in front of him, the two little girls tucked in on either side of her, and the disabled car sitting along the road behind her.

It looked like they had been going through their clothes. Odd. Unless they were planning on taking their clothes and walking to town?

The road was deserted, but it wasn't that deserted. Someone would be along to help them, and if they called, Caleb's Towing would be happy to come get them.

Unless she didn't have any money.

Or, he supposed, it was possible that she didn't have a phone. Although in today's day and age, that was rather unusual.

Michigan was almost all flat and cell service was almost universal, so that couldn't be the problem.

Still, he didn't want to put her off by asking her a bunch of questions, like he was interrogating her. So, he tried to think of the most pertinent question. The one that would determine what he did.

"Are you broken down or just out of gas?" he asked, unable to figure out how to politely say, are you completely out of money?

"Out of gas. I should have gotten some back in Blueberry Beach—"

"But we didn't have any money, and we can't even afford to buy anything to eat." The smaller of the two girls piped up when the woman hesitated.

"I'm sorry." The woman's cheeks turned pink as she took his outstretched hand. "I'm Jubilee, and these are my daughters Scarlett and Penelope. I suppose you should know our names before you know our financial situation."

She was obviously embarrassed.

"Names are nice, but knowing you don't have any money is even more helpful," he said, trying to sound like that was just completely normal information to hand over to a total stranger.

It made him cringe mentally, but he also wanted to smile. Penelope, the girl who had spoken, was very much like his twelve-year-old daughter, Nora. She was rather outspoken as well. Not that he got to spend a lot of time with her. Usually just summers and a few weeks over the holidays. School was going to be out next week, and she'd be with him for a solid three months.

Jubilee looked at her daughter like she wanted to tell her to not say anything else, but it was too late.

"There aren't any hotels in Strawberry Sands, so if you're not here to visit anyone," and he assumed they weren't, otherwise Jubilee would have been calling them already, "I figured I'd take you guys to my mom's place."

There. That was the best way he could figure to say that if she couldn't afford a place to stay, his mom would love to take her in.

"Oh, we couldn't put her out like that."

Of course, that was what she had to say, but Jubilee looked like she sincerely didn't want to put anyone out. She must be at least thirty, but she had an innocence about her that made him want to protect her.

"I know people say you're not putting them out, but I truly mean it. My mom loves company, and she'll just be all over you and your girls. You'll make her day, I promise."

That was the truth. His mom loved taking people in, and Jubilee and her girls were just the kind of people that his mom enjoyed helping. He almost felt like a good Samaritan by bringing the two of them together. Although, he couldn't take credit for Jubilee's car running out of gas.

"Are you sure?" Jubilee asked, biting her lip.

Something about her made him feel a curl of something he hadn't felt for a long time.

He'd messed up when he was a kid, done something stupid, and embarrassed his family. Not that it wasn't something that a million other people had done, but it was a mistake that he would live with for the rest of his life.

Of course, he loved his daughter and wouldn't trade her for the world, but he hated that her upbringing had been the kind of upbringing that he'd never wanted for his child. If he'd been thinking, instead of just feeling and doing what he wanted, not what he knew was right, he wouldn't have made the mistake he did.

It had been a hard lesson, but a good one, he supposed, in a lot of ways, because it had made him become much more deliberate about his life from then until now.

Regardless, he was a little gun-shy when it came to women, because Eva had lied to him. Multiple times, or he probably wouldn't have ended up the way he had, distrustful of any woman not a family member.

"You guys can bring all your suitcases. We'll throw them in the back of my truck, and we'll get you guys in, too. It's just ten minutes or so to my mom's place. She's on Main Street in Strawberry Sands. I assume that's where you're going?" It seemed like the obvious assumption, since that was where the road led. It ended at the lake.

"Yes."

"You don't know anyone there?" he asked, again assuming that she would have called them if she had.

"No. I..." Her cheeks, still pink, darkened even more, and she looked down. "I just have good memories of there. And... I needed somewhere to go... I needed a place to land. A soft place."

He understood about that, even though he'd never left his hometown. It was small, but it was home, and he'd never had the desire to go anywhere else.

She lifted her hand from her suitcase, and he lifted it out, walking up with it and a second one, throwing them in the back of his truck, while Jubilee brought two more bags, and each of her girls handed him a bag.

They went back to their car to get the things in the back seat while Jubilee went and grabbed a few things from the passenger side along with the keys.

"If you give me those, I'll come out tonight or tomorrow and fill it up with gas. I can probably get one of my brothers to bring me out."

"I could do it," she said, biting her lip again, because she was obviously unsure of what tomorrow was going to bring.

"I guess we can cross that bridge when we come to it. If I know my mom, she's going to want to introduce you to everyone and feed you as much as you can eat. If you're really staying and you don't have a job lined up, she's going to want to help find one."

"She sounds like quite a woman," Jubilee said, sounding tired. Like maybe the idea of someone doing all those things made her feel more exhausted than what she already was. "I suppose that's the kind of woman I'd like to be someday," she said, almost as though she were thinking out loud.

He understood how it felt to stand in front of a major mistake and think about all the things that a person wanted out of their life, and all the things they probably weren't going to get, and then about all the ways they were going to try to make their life better and not repeat their mistakes. He didn't know if that was what Jubilee was doing now or not, but it would be what he would be doing.

"She is quite a woman. I didn't appreciate her as much when I was younger, but the older I get, the more I admire her. That's life, right?" He smiled over at her as he put the last bag in the back of his pickup and shut the tailgate.

"You can go ahead and get in if you want." Part of him wanted to go over and open the door for her, but part of him knew that was rather old-fashioned and maybe she would get the wrong idea. The idea that he was a different kind of man than what he actually was.

He was a farmer first, someone who raised hay and horses and leased horses out for tourists during the summer beach season.

They sold some grain on the side as well, and the farm they owned also produced berries and vegetables.

All of them worked with the horses, but he had brothers who were in charge of the other areas of the farm.

Both of the girls walked to the passenger side of the pickup with Jubilee, so Matt walked around his side and got in.

She had the girls in the back and was climbing in on her side as he settled in his seat.

"Do you think it will be okay there?" she asked, looking uneasily at her car.

"I'm sure it will be. You've already seen this road isn't traveled overmuch. If you'd like, it will be almost dark when we get home, but I can come right back out with some gas with one of my brothers."

"I don't want to put you out," she said, although he figured it would ease her mind if that was what he did. After all, as far as he knew, all she had in the world was her car, and if she couldn't even afford to put gas in it, she probably couldn't stand the idea that something might happen to it.

He tried to imagine being that destitute, but he never had been. Plus, he always had his family to stand behind him, to catch him if he fell.

He'd fallen, more than once, although once he'd fallen spectacularly, and while none of his family were happy with him, they supported him nonetheless.

He never doubted that they loved him and that if he needed them, they were there. That was what family was about in his opinion.

This woman, Jubilee, didn't seem to have that. It made him sad. It wasn't just a part of modern America, although maybe it was more prevalent in America today than it used to be, but down through time, there were families who didn't stay together, or who split apart because of differences, or who died, or whatever.

God hadn't seen fit to put him in a family like that, other than his dad leaving when he was a kid, but God had given him the resources to help people who had. He owed that thought to his mother, who had never hesitated to take in anyone who needed it. What a great example she'd been.

"I don't want to be nosy, but is there a reason you're coming to town?" he asked as they pulled out on the highway.

"I'm looking for a job." She hesitated, as though knowing he was going to ask. "But I suppose you want to know why I'm looking in Strawberry Sands, when there's plenty of other places I could be working."

"I guess. Just... Strawberry Sands isn't exactly a hot destination spot for most people. In fact, most people don't even know about it."

"I was here once when I was seventeen. I think I remember you. Did you ride horses along the beach?"

He wasn't expecting that and looked over at her with renewed interest. "My family owns a horse leasing and riding stable. We lease horses to tourists, particularly in the summer. So yeah, I could have been riding my horse along the beach. Did I know you?"

There was one summer where he only had eyes for Eva. Hopefully that wasn't the summer that she remembered him from. It was the one summer he'd like to forget. The memories weren't sweet, more like sour milk. They made him feel guilty and gave him a general sense of unease, because he knew that he let his family down.

"We never talked. I just admired your horse. It was pretty." Jubilee looked out the windshield, like the scenery had changed, which it hadn't. It would be another few miles until they were able to see Lake Michigan, but he understood that. Maybe she was eagerly awaiting the view. He certainly enjoyed it. And the sunset on the lake was absolutely stunning. As long as he lived there, he'd never gotten tired of watching it, and he often stopped what he was doing to spend a few minutes enjoying the play of colors across the sky, to imagine God smiling and feeling content and happy at the enjoyment that His creation got out of the beauty He provided for them.

"My daughter is still in school but should be coming up to spend the summer with me in another week or so. She might be about your oldest daughter's age."

"I am ten," Scarlett piped up, letting him know that she'd been listening to what they were saying. He should have known, since Nora always paid attention to any conversations he was having with his family.

"And I'm eight. She's older than me." Penelope stated the obvious, which made Jubilee smile.

It made Matt smile as well, and they shared a little wordless humor across the seat.

"You just have one daughter?" she asked, showing interest in him for the first time. He wasn't sure why he liked it, but he did.

"Yeah. I'm not married." He didn't usually go around telling everyone everything that he'd ever done in his life, but Jubilee just nodded her head, didn't really say anything, and he continued, naturally, like he was talking to a friend, which was weird. "I don't know what story you have, but there was a summer I ended up doing things I shouldn't have, and I've regretted it ever since, although I don't regret my daughter. She's every bit as amazing as I'm sure you think your kids are, and I look forward to spending the summer with her every year."

"I think we probably all have things we regret," Jubilee said softly, but she didn't elaborate. Which almost made Matt ask about her regrets, although he didn't. Maybe if he prompted her, she would say more, but he didn't want her to have to say more than she wanted to, especially with her daughters sitting right there.

"My whole family was pretty disappointed in me. I'm the oldest, and my mom was really depending on me to set a good example. My dad left when we were little."

"That's too bad. I was actually raised by my aunt. She's gone now."

That's what he thought. That she didn't have much of a homelife. His dad had stuck around long enough for him to acquire six children. Which probably wasn't exactly what his mother wanted, but considering that Matt had five younger siblings and he appreciated each one of them, he was grateful to his dad for that much.

"I don't want to pry, so you don't have to answer me if you don't want, but what about the girls' dad?" he asked, his voice pitched low.

He had grown up without one, and most of the time, he was okay with that, because he knew what kind of man his dad was. A liar and a cheater. He figured he was probably better off without him, but there was still a void.

She glanced behind them where her girls sat, hanging on their every word. "We've been living with his mother, but a couple of days ago, she invited him and his girlfriend over for supper. I decided at that point that it would be a good time for us to head to the lake for a while."

He could read between the lines there. And see that her ex had probably cheated, and she had moved in with his mother, but his mother was firmly on the side of her son, even if her son had blown up his marriage and ruined three other people's lives in the process.

Blood ran deep.

Chapter 3

"It's a mansion!" Penelope exclaimed as they got out of their car and stared at the huge white two-story house with the cute picket fence and the massive old oak tree in the corner of the yard that reminded Jubilee of a 1950s sit-com with the perfect family. The perfect house and perfect life.

That certainly wasn't her. But here she was, being rescued by someone who apparently had grown up in such a thing.

"It's not a mansion, it's a castle," Scarlett, normally the one of her daughters less prone to fantasies, whispered.

"It's just a regular house, although it is much bigger than what we're used to," Jubilee said, trying not to sound as awed as her children.

Matt laughed. "I guess I don't usually see it through the eyes of someone who hasn't before. But maybe that's why my mom has been working on switching it all over to a bed-and-breakfast. There are plenty of bedrooms to go around, especially now that all of her children have moved on."

"You don't live here?" Jubilee asked, then she wished she could take the question back. It shouldn't matter to her where he lived.

"I grew up here. But the farm sprawls all over the northern part of Strawberry Sands. Most of my siblings live around it or on it, just not in the main house. I live down by the stables, in a cottage by the beach. I'm mostly in charge of renting out the horses, and I do a lot with the hay we make, so it makes sense for me to be down there."

"You wanted to live closer to the lake?" Jubilee asked, looking over at the shimmering blue that glowed just below the horizon.

"I guess. Closer to the storms that blow in, but mostly because it was closer to the stables and I'm right there when the tourists come."

"I see," Jubilee said, looking again at the house. It had a beautiful view of the lake. It was huge and had character and just said "family" and seemed so welcoming. She couldn't imagine moving out of it and choosing to live somewhere else, even if it was closer to the shore. But everyone had their different things. Sometimes it seemed like whatever a person had, they wanted something different.

Was that a human trait? A person was never satisfied with what they had but was always looking for something else. Something more. Striving and fighting instead of being content.

"Come on in," Matt said, his hand on the white picket gate. "I texted my mom, and she's expecting us."

"Are you sure that we're not going to be an imposition?" Jubilee bit her lip and tried to keep her fingers from twisting together in front of her. Now that they were here, while she knew she had nowhere else to go, she wished she wouldn't have come.

"I'm sure. Mom will probably try to talk you into moving in and staying forever. She's like that."

Matt had no sooner said that than a slender woman in her fifties pushed open the screen door and stepped out on the front porch.

"Matthew Landry. Why are you standing out there staring at the house? Grab that girl and bring her in here." The woman didn't stop on the porch but bounded down the steps with the bounce of someone much younger than Jubilee had expected Matt's mother to be.

She would have to be in her fifties. Late fifties. And yet, she careened down the steps like a teenager.

"What a terrible thing to have your car break down along the side of the road. That's not exactly a busy highway, and you would have been sitting forever waiting for someone to come." Matt's mom talked as she hurried toward them.

"I hadn't even called anyone because I don't have any money to pay them." Jubilee couldn't see pretending or hiding the truth. If her lack of ability to pay was going to affect whether or not Mrs. Landry wanted to allow them to stay, she wanted to know it now.

"Mom, this is Jubilee. She was planning on moving into Strawberry Sands and getting a job."

"Really?" Mrs. Landry said, looking very interested. More interested than Jubilee would have expected her to look. She wasn't sure what to say about that.

Matt and Mrs. Landry seemed to share a look before Mrs. Landry's attention turned back toward Jubilee.

"Jubilee, this is my mom, Lana."

"Such a pleasure to meet you, Mrs. Landry," Jubilee said, holding out her hand.

"Please, call me Lana. When my husband walked out on me, I almost changed my name back to my maiden name. But with six kids, it would have been a real paperwork nightmare to change everyone's, and I didn't really want to kick the sleeping giant, if you know what I mean." Lana grinned a little, and Jubilee found herself grinning back. She knew all about that. Sometimes it was better to just live and let live, and not do things deliberately, things that one knew was going to make someone else mad. Even if they were things that someone wanted to do.

"I have some experience in that," Jubilee said, feeling an immediate kinship with Lana that she hadn't before as the older woman gripped her hand in her own callused palm and gave it a firm shake.

"These are my daughters, Scarlett and Penelope," Jubilee said as she pulled her hand back.

"Well, hello, girls. I hope you're going to talk your mom into staying for a while. After all, that tire swing out there hasn't been used in a really long time, and I'd love it if I had two little girls to try it out to make sure it still works."

"Can we do it now?" Penelope asked, her brows lifted, her look eager.

"There are a lot of other things around here that need a child's touch once in a while. So hopefully you're going to get your mom to stay."

"I already told you I can't pay you," Jubilee said, giving her head a slight shake as Penelope continued to look at her with pleading eyes.

"And I told you you didn't have to worry about that," Matt said, his voice firm. "Mom, where would you like their luggage?"

"Just hold on a second. She hasn't invited us to stay, and I haven't said that I would." Jubilee felt like she was losing control of the situation, that Matt was going to strong-arm his mother into allowing her to stay and strong-arm her into imposing.

"Matt just knows me really well. Anyone who comes is welcome. I'm sorry I didn't say that right away. And I certainly don't expect payment. Not from someone whose car is broken down and we're doing a good deed for. After all, if you pay me now, God won't be able to pay me in heaven. And I'd rather have the heavenly cash."

Jubilee froze for a moment, listening to what Lana said. She'd been around Christians all of her life. Of course. And she considered herself one, too. But she'd never heard of someone refusing money because they wanted "heavenly cash." That was new. But...should it be true? The Bible did say if you got reward on earth, you wouldn't get it in heaven. And it stood to reason that the heavenly payment would be much better than the earthly one.

"Are you convinced now?" Matt said, and there was a note in his voice, one that made her think that he cared.

She tried to ignore that too. There were just too many things happening, too many nice things. She wasn't used to it all.

"Are you trying to get me to tell you that you were right?" she asked, turning to him and lifting her brows. She didn't want to admit that, but at the same time...

"I'm sorry, I know that sometimes Matt can be a little overbearing and bossy. That's the tendency of the firstborn, isn't it?" Lana laughed like there was nothing she could do about it. And there probably wasn't. "But he also makes a great packhorse, which maybe isn't as much of a tendency of the firstborn as it is of big, strapping guys who do a lot of work outside. Go ahead and bring her stuff in, and put her in the last bedroom on the right at the top of the stairs." She smiled and looked at Jubilee. "That's the biggest one, and it has a bathroom attached. It also is directly across from the bedroom that has bunk beds in it where I think your girls will be most comfortable."

"Bunk beds?" Penelope asked, again looking excited.

This whole unexpected breakdown was proving to be the most excitement and happiness her girls had in a long time.

"Yes. Bunk beds, and they're blue and red—blueberries and strawberries. Perfect for both of you, I think," Lana said, winking at Jubilee.

Her girls were both young enough to appreciate bunk beds in a blue and red room. Especially one that might look like berries.

"How about I lead you up and I'll show you both your rooms, and we'll let Matt do his packhorsing duties."

Lana didn't seem to have a problem leaving Matt to do all the work, but it bothered Jubilee. She wasn't used to people serving her. So she said, "I'll give him a hand."

Lana gave a knowing look, like it didn't surprise her that Jubilee wanted to help. "Is it okay if I take the girls up?"

"It sure is." They were both carrying the packs that they had to keep them entertained in the car. That would be enough for them to carry.

Lana disappeared in the house while Jubilee turned back toward the truck where Matt was already rummaging around in the back.

"You know, I'm a little insulted that you don't think I can carry this," he said casually as he lifted the suitcase out of the back of his truck and set it on the ground, turning to grab another.

"It wasn't that I didn't think you could. It's just that I didn't think I could just stand around while someone else did all of my work for me."

He grunted a little and didn't say anything while he pulled the other suitcase out. "I guess I get that. I wouldn't want to stand around either."

She got to the front of the truck and grabbed the overnight bag she packed, as well as several other little bags.

"You know, my mom really is happy to have visitors. I think since all her kids moved out, she's lonely. So, I just wanted you to know she's not the kind of person to put on a show for no reason. If she says she's happy to have you, she means it." Matt's voice was low, and it almost seemed to Jubilee like he was trying to talk her into being a friend to his mom.

His mom didn't strike her as the kind of person who had trouble making friends or who had trouble keeping herself occupied. But Jubilee kept that to herself and just thought about how cute it was that Matt was concerned about his mother. It wasn't something that she typically thought of men doing—thinking about how their mom might feel.

She already admired Matt way too much, she didn't need to think about that as well. So she shoved the thought aside, slung the bags over her shoulders, and grabbed a suitcase, starting toward the house.

"Hey. Leave some things for me to carry," he complained as he took the smaller of the two suitcases and the last bag.

"It's my stuff. I should take the brunt of it."

"I'm bigger than you are, and I'm stronger. I should put those muscles to use."

She just laughed and shook her head. She could argue with him about it, but they both had legitimate points.

"I'll let you lead the way, since you know which room your mom was talking about."

He gave her a look that said he was letting her win, which caused her to shrug and give him a smirky smile that said she knew she could rub it in but she was choosing not to.

There was so much about Matt that she liked, and it was surprising how comfortable she felt with him. Especially considering what she'd just been through with her ex. She needed to be careful.

Chapter 4

"Do you think she'd like a job here?" Lana settled on the porch swing that evening.

Matt had gone after Jubilee's car with his brother Luke. They'd filled it up with gas and brought it back. Luke had stayed along with Matt and Sunday, her daughter who lived the closest. The three of them were on the porch with her now.

"Jubilee?" Matt's voice came out of the darkness from where he stood leaning against the porch post, looking out toward the horizon and the lake that shimmered with moonlight.

"Yes," Lana said, thinking that it was obvious, but maybe Matt just wanted to be sure. Or maybe he was thinking about something else. His daughter was set to arrive soon. Maybe he was thinking about that. It was hard to tell, and Lana tried to stop worrying about it. Matt's life was his, and if he wanted help with that, he could ask.

"I think she's a godsend. You needed someone, and there she is," Sunday said from her position beside Lana on the porch swing. Sunday had just come back to Strawberry Sands and was working on breeding warmbloods. It had been her dream all of her life, although she'd gotten sidetracked with a few things. She was back on track now.

"I say Sunday's right," Luke's voice came from the step where he sat with his arm resting on his leg, his dog at his feet. He didn't go anywhere without Rocky.

"All right. I don't think we necessarily have to take a family vote on it. After all, it's mostly up to me. Since the bed-and-breakfast is pretty much my baby. But you guys give me a hand, and I didn't want to disrespect anyone by not talking to you about it first." She mostly wanted to know Matt's opinion. He seemed...not taken exactly with Jubilee, but...interested.

Maybe that was just her mother's heart hoping that her son would finally find someone he could settle down and be happy with.

"Mom, you don't have to ask us. We'll give you a hand no matter what you do. We just want you to be happy. After what you went through with Dad, you deserve it."

"I don't deserve anything but hell. Although, I do appreciate you saying so. That's sweet." She wanted to be clear about that. She didn't walk around thinking that because her husband had cheated and left her, and taken as much as he could from her, and still made her life miserable on occasion, it meant that she deserved anything more than anyone else. God expected her to take whatever He had given her in this life and make the best of it.

Of course, she reminded herself over and over again that she had chosen her husband. No one had forced her to marry him. She had no idea that he wasn't going to be a man of his word. That he was going to lie and break promises and cheat, but that didn't change the fact that he had been her choice.

Matt grunted. "I will feel better if you have someone here. Last summer, you worked yourself ragged, and the bed-and-breakfast wasn't even that full."

"Strawberry Sands is growing. New people are coming into town as Blueberry Beach gets bigger and bigger. With the riding stable and now the diner, especially with Griff's strawberry creations, there are a lot of things happening here that weren't happening last year. I agree with Matt. You need the help." Luke was quieter, the steady brother. To have his vote of confidence meant a lot to her.

"All right. I'll see what she says in the morning. Did you hear anything else from her?" she asked, mostly talking to Matt. Sunday hadn't come until after they'd gone to bed, and the same for Luke. Matt hadn't eaten supper with them, but he talked to her some in his truck on the way here.

"Not really." And that's all he said. Funny that sometimes the boys could talk up a storm, and other times trying to pry information from them was like trying to pry orange juice from a feather.

Lana slept on it, like she liked to do, and prayed about it too. She just had a feeling about Jubilee. She wasn't sure exactly what it was about her, but she just felt like she needed to help her. So, when she was standing in the kitchen the next morning, and Jubilee poked her head in the doorway, Lana decided that it was time to lay their cards on the table.

"Good morning," she said with a smile, nodding at the fruit bowl on the counter. "There's fruit, and if you'd like to make yourself some oatmeal or some eggs, you can help yourself to whatever."

"Maybe I'll wait until my kids get up."

"There's cereal in the pantry if that's what they like."

"I'm sure that's probably what they prefer, but I might cook eggs if that's okay. I'll cook some for you?"

"I'm not usually too hungry first thing in the morning, but I was kind of hoping we could talk if you have a minute?" Lana asked, taking her banana and her coffee and nodding at the back patio.

"I'd love to. I actually laid awake last night thinking that I'd like to talk to you."

"Well, that makes two of us." Lana smiled as she used her elbow to unlatch the door and push it open.

Back years ago, when they farmed the ground as a family, she started working as soon as her feet hit the floor in the morning and didn't stop until dark or after. There were very few slow, peaceful mornings and even fewer of those kinds of days.

"A lovely morning. It's my favorite time," she said as the rising sun cast a glow over the lake.

Their house faced the street so they could see the lake from the ends of both the front and back porches. Sometimes she wondered why the house was set up like that; after all, a beautiful view of the lake from the front porch would be ideal. But she had to admit that she liked the fact that she could see it from either porch. Maybe that was the better way to build it.

"So you didn't sleep very well?" she asked as Jubilee got settled in a chair.

"No. I guess I didn't. But it wasn't that there was anything wrong with the room. I loved it. Beautifully decorated, and the bed was so comfortable."

"Thanks. Clara helped me decorate the house. She loves that kind of thing. She's always wanted to open up her own artist shop by the beach, but she fears that it would be a failure, and I think she's afraid to just step out and try. You know?"

"Well, failing isn't fun," Jubilee said reasonably. "I guess I don't blame her." She sighed. "I wouldn't be here if I hadn't failed in my marriage."

"That leaves a person with a really bad sense of not being able to do anything right, doesn't it?"

"Yeah," Jubilee said, her posture slumped, but her eyes brightening just a tad like she hadn't considered that Lana might have experience in that too.

Lana didn't usually share her story. But before she thought about it, her mouth opened. "We used to farm this. We had five hundred acres. The boys did hay with their dad. The girls and I helped. We had a big vegetable operation as well and twenty acres devoted to blueberries. But winters are long and dark and hard, and there's a lot of women dressed in a lot of nothing on the beach in the summer that look pretty tempt-

ing to a man with no morals. My husband...cheated a lot before he finally
left."

"That's sad."

"Yeah. It was devastating. I suspected
for years that he might not be completely true. You know, overhearing the
odd conversation, seeing a text on his
phone, where he said he was going
didn't quite line up with where I heard
he was. Those kinds of things. But you
can't really follow after your husband,
demanding that he explain every single
thing that he's ever done, because then
you look like an overbearing, nagging,
and paranoid wife, don't you?"

"You do. Even if you're justified in your
fears. Although, even if you're not justi-

fied in your fears, it shouldn't hurt to ask. Right? If there's nothing going on, then your husband shouldn't have a problem answering a simple question of 'you said you were going to be here, why did I hear that you were there?'"

Lana nodded, seeing that Jubilee understood exactly what she was saying.

"Anyway, that was tough. And we sold a little bit of land, just to try to make ends meet and to pay off the rest of the farm. I wish I wouldn't have had to do that now, because with six kids, I could have used that. But that's just what I had to do."

"Then you do really understand the idea of starting over."

"I do."

"Do you know of any places in town that are hiring? I mean, I know that Blueberry Beach is a lot bigger, and I could find a job there, but I know that housing would be more expensive there as well."

"There isn't a whole lot of housing here, but I talked to Matt and one of his brothers, Luke. Sunday, one of my three daughters, was here as well last night. I don't exactly need my kids' permission to do anything, but I had this idea, and it involves you."

"Okay," Jubilee said, pushing one strand of brown hair that had been loosened by the wind back behind her ear.

"I think Matt told you that I run a bed-and-breakfast here?"

"He did."

"It's going to be busy by the end of this month, and for July and August as well. I… I can handle the guests, and cooking breakfast, making meals, even the cleaning is not too bad. But I've been trying to do an organic garden to go along with it. People enjoy eating fresh fruits and vegetables, and they love it whenever what is served is grown right here on the farm. I… I get behind in the gardening. And I was wondering if you would help me with that, especially. But with anything else that I need help with as well. With eight bedrooms and a mother-in-law suite in the basement, it gets to be a lot. And that was last year. I'm going to be a lot busier this year."

"You want to give me a job?" Jubilee asked, and she sounded like she couldn't believe it.

"I do. I... I think I could even keep you on definitely in the spring and fall, and possibly even the winter if we get booked over Christmas. Which happened to my surprise last year. I wasn't expecting that."

"I think lots of people want to get away for Christmas. It's easier to let someone else clean after you're done than to do it yourself. Or maybe it's just the idea of everyone meets at someone else's house."

"Exactly. Whatever it is, it was a big deal, and I was actually fully booked for almost the entire month of December."

"There might even be a way to frame it so that people want to come to the lake in January and February. There would be skiing here and ice fishing."

"We did have some ice fishermen. And I suppose if there were a ski shop... I suppose we should have a surf shop in Strawberry Sands before we have a ski shop." They laughed together.

"It could be both. You know, in the summer a surf shop, in the winter a ski shop, with the merchandise flipping back and forth from the back to the front of the store."

"Someone needs to do that."

"Maybe we should," Jubilee said, laughing, but Lana sobered immediately.

"Why don't we?" she asked.

Jubilee's mouth opened and closed like she was thinking about all the reasons why they shouldn't.

The first probably being that they just met yesterday, they could hardly go into business together when they didn't even know each other.

Rather than let Jubilee stew, Lana just started talking. "I hadn't considered that at all, and I don't know much about surfing. Or skiing for that matter, but it could end up being great for my bed-and-breakfast business, so I could look into it. It would be something to do in the winter. It would give an added income. If we are careful with our expenses, we should at least break even. There is an empty store, several actually, right on Main Street in Strawberry Sands. Not far from the beach. The horses are a big draw up here, and maybe we could add saddles and other horse paraphernalia as well."

"You're serious," Jubilee said, and she still sounded surprised.

"Yes. I want to say, let's do this. Because I am serious, but I understand that you're just coming from a huge change, and we did just meet each other. Let's work to-gether for the summer. Let's think about it. Let's see what happens, and let's keep that in mind. It might be something that we want to do for the long haul."

"I'm kind of in disbelief, but yeah. I... I could really get into that. I want to settle somewhere and put down roots."

"You don't have to tell me what happened to make you feel like you need a change, but if you want to, I can listen." Lana thought that maybe she should have started with that. She just didn't want to pry too hard into Jubilee's background and make her feel defensive or insecure.

"I guess everybody who's divorced has a story like that. A cheating husband or some way they just couldn't get along. I guess... I guess mine's the same. Although sometimes I think that I can't really blame everything on my husband. I made mistakes too. You know?"

"I think there's a difference between making mistakes, which is human nature, and cheating or abuse."

"There wasn't any abuse. No physical abuse anyway. But I couldn't stay with a man I couldn't trust after he cheated. And I just had to go."

"And you picked Strawberry Sands?"

"I had great memories here. We spent the summer here. It was the best summer of my life. I felt the pull and wanted to come back. I guess we always want to go where we have the happy memories. The places that made us feel secure. That's what Strawberry Sands is to me." She laughed a little. "I guess it was pretty interesting to me that when I broke down, Matt was the one who found me.

He wasn't someone I hung out with that summer, but he was someone I admired from a distance. I'm sure you know he's good looking."

"He's my son. Of course I think he's good looking. But his dad was really good looking too. I think that was probably the problem. Maybe Matt knows that, he…made a mistake back when he was younger. And I think he worries that his looks attract the wrong kind of women. Or maybe he just doesn't know how to tell the difference between the right and wrong kinds."

"He said something about his daughter coming for the summer."

"Yeah. That's probably his story to tell, but that was what I was talking about.

Her mother was...not the right kind of woman." Lana sighed. She didn't want to bad-mouth Eva. Although, some people grew up, and some people just didn't. "Everyone can change. Everyone makes mistakes. Sometimes we look at someone and they've done something, and we don't ever want to give them credit for becoming someone different. You know?"

"I'm not the same person I used to be. But sometimes I want to look at someone else and think that they couldn't possibly change. I look for proof of that, you know? And you can always find proof."

"Exactly. You really can. I'm guilty of that too. After all, I know the pain that Matt has been through, and I suppose that makes me even more protective, since he's my son. Anyway, Nora, his daughter who is twelve, about the same age as Scarlett if I'm not mistaken, will be here in a week or so."

"Will there be enough room in the house for her too?"

"She usually stays with Matt. So we don't need to worry about that. Although, as my granddaughter, I do like to have overnights with her." Lana smiled, thinking about the good times that she had with Nora over the years. "Sometimes I wish I saw her more than just in the summer, but the summer is the best time to be here by the lake, so I just try to focus on that."

"I guess we have to focus on the good. After all, if we don't, we could get sucked down into a huge depression."

"Once you're down, it's so hard to pull yourself back up. Because what you have to do is get a hold of your thoughts and shift them. Which is not an easy thing to do."

"Why is it so much easier to think about negative things than it is to think about positive things?" Jubilee asked, like that was a question that she wondered about before.

"I'm not sure. But it seems to be a struggle we have our whole lives."

"I guess my first thought about it being crazy to think about a surf and ski shop was negative thinking. And the idea that you had about your daughter who wanted to open an art studio but was afraid. Maybe we should think really hard about that, because it's like I said, what does it matter if you fail? Isn't that life?"

"Exactly," Lina said, smiling. Jubilee was even more than what she thought. The idea caused a little bubble of excitement to form in her chest. It was almost as though she could feel the hand of the Lord working.

Chapter 5

Matt finished brushing Boots, his chestnut gelding, and straightened, his hand on Boots's neck, looking out over the lake.

He'd enjoyed a beautiful early morning ride, watching the sunrise reflect off the water and feeling the breeze on his face, still chilly, despite the fact that it was June.

Soon his daughter would be there to spend the summer with him, and they'd take early morning horse rides together. Nora had always loved riding, and he never had to wake her up.

A part of him said that maybe things would be different this year. She'd be twelve, and that was a hard age for many kids, but a part of him wanted to believe that she would be just the way she was forever. A little girl who was happy and cheerful and loved everything.

Unlike her mother.

He patted Boots's neck and then un-hooked the lead from the hitching post, leading Boots back into the barn. Unfor-tunately, both of them had to start their day, as much as he loved spending the morning out in the wide-open air, talking to the Lord, and adjusting his thoughts for the day.

As he turned, movement caught his eye, and he saw a car rolling into his drive up over the hill and down the other side.

After a second or two of confusion, he thought he recognized Eva's car. His...ex was here? He wasn't sure he could call her that. They hadn't really even dated. They'd just spent a few weeks of one fateful summer together, and done things they shouldn't have, and ended up with a child.

It had totally derailed everything he thought about himself and everything he thought he was going to do with his life.

He hadn't ever thought that he would be the kind of person who did the things he had done.

It had sent him into a bit of a faith crisis.

It ended up being a good thing, because he had come out of it more grounded in his beliefs than he ever had before, but it had definitely changed him. He loved Nora and wouldn't trade her for the world, but so many times he wished he could go back and do that summer over.

He would have had a lot more barriers up. He'd always kind of laughed when his mom had warned him about doing things that everyone else did. Kissing, holding hands, silly things that were totally innocent. Except, they led to other things that weren't so innocent. And at some point, one had to draw the line. His mom had always suggested that he draw the line at not even starting, and then he didn't have to wonder and worry about where to stop.

In hindsight, that advice was spot on.

But as a teen, he thought it was silly. He thought he knew what was right and what was wrong, and he wouldn't have a problem making sure he only did what was right. Except, what was wrong was so tempting.

And he had been with a girl who didn't have any compunctions at all about being intimate before marriage.

The warnings that his mom had given him about not dating girls that weren't

Christians had totally gone in one ear and out the other. It seemed a little judgy to only want to date people who believed the way he did. After all, that was cutting out about eighty percent of the dating pool. And he didn't want that. All the good-looking girls, all the girls who wore short shorts and skimpy tops, were pretty much in the eighty percent who didn't go to church.

He'd determined in his heart that he wasn't going to make that mistake again.

And he'd done everything he could to do right by Eva and Nora.

They agreed that he got Nora in the summer and two weeks around Christmas time, and occasionally for other holidays. Normally Eva and he talked about it and he knew when to expect them. This year, Eva hadn't said anything. He assumed the end of the school year was busy—he'd already driven to Indiana twice to see Nora in several productions and awards ceremonies. But as he watched the car pull to a stop, he was certain it was Eva in the driver seat with Nora's blonde head bobbing around on the passenger side.

Opening the gate, he put Boots in the side pasture, unhooked the lead, and watched him kick up his heels, then gallop twenty yards before dropping and rolling.

So much for all the brushing he'd just done.

He walked back around the barn, hung the lead on a hook, and then walked toward the cottage where he stayed. Nora and Eva were both out of the car and had walked to the trunk, grabbing Nora's things.

Seemed like she had a lot more things than usual.

"Hey there, kiddo," he said, going around the car and putting a hand on Nora's shoulder.

"Dad!" Nora said, turning and throwing her arms around him. "I didn't think you'd be back from your ride yet."

"I was just brushing Boots down. If I had known you were coming, I would have waited and we could have taken a ride together."

"Maybe later. Tonight if it's not too hot."

"I don't think it's going to be that bad; there's a nice breeze today."

He lifted his eyes, meeting Eva's over the top of Nora's head. Her eyes skittered away. "I guess I missed your text to say that you were coming."

"Mom said we were going to surprise you. She let me skip the last four days of school."

"She did?" Matt said, unable to keep the surprise out of his voice. Eva hadn't said anything about that. He wasn't sure he approved. Although he had to admit that he'd allowed all responsibility for the schooling to fall on Eva's shoulders. He typically showed up for anything they invited him to, of course, Christmas concerts, plays, and programs, but as for making sure that Nora did her schoolwork or that she studied for tests or anything like that, it was all on Eva's shoulders.

He didn't like that, but it wasn't necessarily something he could control. After all, because he wasn't married to Eva, because Nora had to be shuffled back and forth between the two houses, there had to be a few things that weren't ideal. That was one of them.

Still, Eva wasn't meeting his eyes. Usually she dropped Nora off, said a few words, and tore out of town as fast as she could.

"Hello, Eva," he finally said while she busied herself in the trunk and didn't look up.

"Matt. I'm sorry we didn't give you any warning, although it's not like you have anyone to look after other than yourself." Maybe she didn't mean that the way it sounded. "I decided I was coming to Strawberry Sands for the summer."

That was new.

Matt tried to contain his...consternation.

"Nora, honey. Want to grab your stuff and run in and put it in your room? I got everything ready so that you and your dad can take it right in to your bedroom."

So she was getting Nora out of the way so she could tell him whatever was going on. It must be worse than what he thought.

He helped Nora lift her bag out of the trunk and start her suitcase rolling on the sand. Once she had it on the porch, it would roll easier, and he was tempted to help her, but he was curious too.

Dark eyes, and two little girls who were as adorable as they could be, flittered through his head. For some reason, he'd been thinking that when Nora came, she would enjoy playing with Jubilee's girls. He had been thinking that the summer would be spent at his mom's house, and Jubilee's girls would play with Nora while he... He wasn't even sure what he was going to do, but it would involve Jubilee. She had been on his mind since he picked her up yesterday and brought her to his mom's house.

"I need to talk to you, Matt," Eva said as soon as Nora disappeared inside his cottage.

"All right. I kinda figured you did since you sent Nora away."

"I left George. I need a place to stay. I was hoping I could crash in your extra bedroom."

No. He was absolutely not letting his...whatever Eva was...stay at his house. Sure, they shared a child together, but there was no way he was even going to give the appearance of any kind of relationship between them to anyone.

"You don't have anywhere else?" he asked carefully, fighting back the absolute refusal that wanted to pop out of his mouth.

"I'll have money once we get the divorce settled, but I don't know how long that'll take. I've never filed for divorce before."

After she had Nora, she'd lived with a guy for a couple of years after she moved to Chicago. Then, when she moved to Indiana, she and George set up house together. They married after living together for a year or so.

"I don't really know either." A couple of his siblings had gotten divorced, but he'd never gotten sucked up in the details, just knew that divorce was hard on everyone involved. But when a spouse was unfaithful, when they didn't seem to be sorry and refused to apologize or to make changes to make sure that the unfaithfulness didn't happen again, to be sure trust was restored in the relationship, there didn't seem to be much choice. Unfortunately.

"George cheated on you?" he said, pulling the last suitcase out of the back of the car and closing the trunk.

"No. George is George. Totally dependable. But he's just boring. I wanted something…different. I guess I got nostalgic for Strawberry Sands and the way we used to walk on the beach. Don't you remember that?"

He hoped she wasn't saying she was nostalgic for him. "Yeah. I remember that. We ended up with a child that neither one of us were ready for. So, I limit my walking on the beach to horses, unless

I'm interested in being a lot more with someone than a casual friend."

"Oh, Matt. You were always such a prude. I thought for sure you'd gotten over that by now." Eva rolled her eyes as she put her hands on her hips and looked out toward the lake. "Surely we're old enough to be adults about every-thing. And you do know there is such a thing as birth control. Both of us should have been using it back then. Neither one of us were smart enough."

The tone of her voice was irritated and disgusted. Like she was blaming their lack of birth control for everything that happened, where he blamed their lack of boundaries to begin with. And the idea that there was a moral code given by their Creator that they violated.

"Anyway, that's all in the past. Although... I think we probably would have been really good together. Why didn't we get married again?" She tilted her head and smiled a little as though she were flirting with him.

"Because we really didn't like each other," he said flatly. And that was true. She considered him a prude and didn't really like anything about him other than his apparently handsome face.

Maybe the way he looked in his board shorts.

"Oh, stop. You were a little bit too conservative for me, but you've loosened up over the years. Nora says you even walk in your bare feet on the beach. That's an improvement."

"I walked in my bare feet back then." It didn't make any sense to him, nothing Eva said ever did. She just seemed a little bit...vapid. Not that he was a deep intellectual or anything, he just liked to have a little bit more substance to his conversations. At least, now that he was older, he did. Apparently when he was twenty, he was less interested in talking and more interested in doing other things.

"My mom has an extra room that's not booked right now. And I don't think anyone's booking her mother-in-law suite that's down in the basement. You might be able to get either one of those two, and I'm sure she'll give you a discount." His mom would probably be thrilled that Eva was there for the summer. Just because it would be nice for Nora to have both of her parents together. It seemed like a kid always enjoyed having the two people who loved them best in the world together with them. There was something hardwired in a kid that wanted a family that way.

For what felt like the millionth time, Matt kicked himself for being such an idiot. Because of his idiotic mistakes, Nora hadn't had what every kid wanted—a family.

"Are you serious?" Eva said, and now she didn't have any problems spearing him with her sharp green gaze. Her eyes were narrow, and her lips flat. "Are you really not going to let the mother of your child stay in your cottage for just a few weeks?"

"You said you wanted to stay for the summer."

"That's just a few weeks. By the time we turn around, it's going to be September and time for school to start again."

"That's three months. And no. I probably would let you stay overnight, if it were necessary, but yeah, check with my mom. In fact, if you need me to pay for your room, I can do that."

"Gee. Thanks. You're so generous." Sarcasm was heavy in her voice.

"Eva. Let's not fight about this. You know as well as I do that you can't stay in my house. It would look like we're living together. And it's important to me that I keep a reputation of being honest and upright, mostly because of Nora. I haven't done the best for her, and that's one thing I can do—give her a good name." The Bible talked about how having a good name was important. For Matt, he didn't really care what people thought, unless it went against the Bible. Since God cared, Matt did, too.

"A good name in your circles. But the rest of the world doesn't give a crap." Eva was obviously still upset.

"I guess you're right. But I don't live my life based on what the rest of the world thinks. I want to live it based on what God thinks." Eva had never understood that. And he supposed he was wasting his breath talking to her now. But he did feel a little bit bad since she had obviously been planning on staying with him.

"You can set that suitcase back in the car. I'll go see what your mom says." Eva crossed her arms over her chest after she opened the trunk for him.

He lifted it back up and set it back in. "If Mom has suddenly gotten booked overnight, I'll help you find somewhere else." That was the best he could do.

Suddenly he realized Jubilee was staying with his mom, and if Eva found a room there, they'd be staying together. His ex and...Jubilee. He didn't even know what to call Jubilee. She certainly wasn't a girl-friend, not even close. He didn't know if he wanted her to be. He just knew there was something about her that made his heart feel a little lighter. A little happier. There was a pull there that made him want to be with her. Some kind of obsession, maybe that was too strong of a word, but something that made her image flow through his brain at the oddest times, that made him want to think about her when he should most definitely be thinking about something else. Like getting rid of Eva and making sure she wasn't staying at his mom's house. And thinking about how he shouldn't offer that to her.

But it was too late.

"All right. I'll be in touch with Nora. I'll let her know where I'm staying, and I'm sure she'd like it if we can do a few things together." Eva's voice held less warmth than it had when she had arrived, almost like she had been expecting to talk to him and take up with him now that she wasn't with her husband anymore. Maybe that wasn't what she was thinking, but maybe she was going to butter him up so he would let her stay at his house.

He wasn't sure. He'd never been very good at figuring women out. The only thing he could say for almost certain was that Eva had been expecting something from him, and now she was pretty sure she wasn't getting it.

At least they'd gotten that much settled.

Chapter 6

"I promise you when it comes out of the oven, you will never even be able to taste the zucchini in it." Lana winked at Jubilee as she put the pans of chocolate zucchini bread in the oven.

Her girls had helped and were now standing at the sink working on scrubbing the dishes.

Lana had said after a full morning of work, they should go down to the lake and at least play in the waves a bit and cool off before they came back up and worked in the garden in the evening.

Her girls were all for that. And Jubilee had agreed that once this chocolate zucchini bread was out of the oven, she would deliver two loaves to Kim and Davis Thatcher who had just gotten out of the NICU with their brand-new daughter.

Jubilee hadn't met them yet, but delivering chocolate zucchini bread seemed like a good way to meet the neighbors. Then she and her girls would go down to the lake for a bit before they came back up to work a little more. She liked the easy, relaxed way that Lana did things. There was no stress or striving, just consistent work, with a lot of emphasis on laughing and having fun while things got done.

It was an inspiration to Jubilee and a way of living that she hoped to pick up.

A knock at the door interrupted their conversation.

It opened before either of them could leave the kitchen, and they heard footsteps in the hall.

"We're back here," Lana called, drying her hands on a dish towel while Jubilee set the timer on the oven.

She had a hard time believing that the chocolate zucchini bread would taste just like chocolate cake, but Lana hadn't lied to her yet. In fact, Lana had been far better to her than she deserved. A single mom with absolutely no money. Lana had taken her under her wing and treated her like she was doing Lana a favor by agreeing to work for her.

"Eva," Lana said, sounding surprised.

Jubilee turned. The woman standing in front of her was a little chunky, with short, spiky hair and a hard edge to her face. She was obviously familiar to Lana.

She had a little diamond stud in one nostril and a tattoo of a dragon that snaked up her left arm. The muscle shirt she wore showed it off the whole way to her shoulder.

"Lana. In the kitchen as always. Little Betty homemaker," the lady said with a bit of a smirk. Then her eyes landed on Jubilee who had turned from the oven and grabbed the dishrag to wipe the counter.

"So you already hired help for the summer?" she asked, without introducing herself.

"Eva, this is Jubilee. And her two daughters, Scarlett and Penelope. They're about the same age as Nora. Maybe they'll be playmates this summer."

"They look a little younger than Nora. Nora's very mature for her age," Eva said, neither returning Lana's smile nor responding to the invitation of playdates for their girls.

Jubilee wasn't quite sure what the tension in the air was from, but she suspected that there was more to Eva than met the eye.

"Nora is one of my grandchildren. Matt's daughter," Lana said, turning to Jubilee and telling her in a voice that wasn't quite as full of fun and friendship as it had been before. It seemed like there was a bit of stress in it.

"I'm Matt's dirty little secret," Eva said, wrinkling her face up into a not-quite smirk.

"I see. I guess it was a very good secret, since I didn't know about it. I just started yesterday, though, so I suppose that's why." Jubilee didn't really know what else to say. Eva didn't seem to be in the kitchen trying to make friends.

"I asked Matt if I could stay at his cottage, since you might as well know I left my husband. He's just a big stick-in-the-mud. Never wants to do any-thing fun, and gets all upset if I do." She rolled her eyes. "Anyway, I'll be getting a divorce settlement at some point, but until then, I need a place to stay. Like I said, Matt's a prude. And he doesn't want me staying with him. He suggested I find a place here." She looked at Jubilee like Jubilee was standing in her way of having a beautiful summer home.

"If you need me to move out of my room—"

"Of course not. That's yours. And that's final." Lana turned back toward Eva. "I have a mother-in-law suite in the base-ment if you'd like that. It has everything you need. It's like a studio apartment. I mean, I assume Nora is still staying with Matt?"

"That's the agreement. Nora wouldn't think of staying anywhere else. She just thinks the beach cottage is the best. Some of us have to work for what we get," Eva said, and there was an eye roll in the tone of her voice.

Like somehow Matt didn't work to earn what he had.

"We weren't all born on farms."

Jubilee tried to focus on cleaning the counters and was grateful that her daughters were both quiet. Obviously there was some bad blood somewhere, or maybe Eva just walked around with a chip on her shoulder.

"Anyway. I'll take you up on that. Unless Matt relents and lets me stay at his house. He told me he thought it wouldn't look good if he and I were living together." She put her fingers up and did air quotes around "living together," like it was obvious that they wouldn't be doing anything other than staying in the same house. And that living together implied a lot more.

Jubilee wished she and her girls were out of the kitchen, because it seemed like there was so much tension radiating off Eva, and it made her nervous. She didn't like it when people couldn't get along. She'd much rather have smooth sailing, which was probably normal and something everyone wanted.

But of course, that wasn't the way life worked out for most people, and sometimes, all people needed was someone to be friendly to them.

"If you decide that your daughter might want to spend some time with my girls, we could have a beach day together," she said, unable to come up with any other idea of anything to say.

"Oh, I think Nora would love—"

"Most of the time when Nora's here, she spends her days with Matt. That's the agreement. He gets her in the summer and two weeks at Christmas. I get her the rest of the time. Knowing Matt, if I tried to take Nora to have a beach day with friends, he'd complain that I was taking her from him."

"All right," Jubilee said, unsure what else to say.

"Do you need help carrying your things in?" she finally asked, wishing the zucchini bread would hurry up and get done.

"Actually, that'd be great. Since I don't think there's an outside entrance to the mother-in-law suite in the basement, is there?" Eva asked, turning toward Lana.

"Nope. You have to come in through the house. The kitchen door's the best door to come through, because the steps are right there. But the front door is always open, as you know."

"They want to relegate me to the basement. The dungeon. I'm not what their family is proud of. They're all goody-two-shoes Christians, and I'm just the big reminder that Matt screwed up and had sex before he was married." She looked over her shoulder. "Am I allowed to say sex in this house?" she asked Lana.

"I don't think you're shocking anyone, but sometimes what we're allowed to say and what's prudent to say are two different things," Lana said, still sounding friendly, but there was a chill in her tone that Jubilee noticed right away. She didn't like someone making fun of her Christian values. Maybe it was because of the girls standing at the sink. After all, if they were exposed to people who mocked their faith, it was possible that they might start to question why they would stay with it, especially when everyone made fun of them. It was a dangerous thing when a kid wasn't sure if their foundation was secure.

It took a strong person to continue to stand for what they believed when everyone around them tried to convince them that they were prudish and old-fashioned.

Eva didn't talk much as they walked out to the car, grabbed two large, heavy suitcases, and rolled them up the walk.

"Are you staying here for the summer?" Eva asked as they lifted the suitcases up the front steps, one step at a time.

"At least. I was thinking about staying here forever. But I'll have to find a place to stay, since I can't keep taking advantage of Lana's generosity."

"Whatever room you're staying in, you'll be taking money out of her pocket since she can't rent it out."

"Does she normally rent out the mother-in-law suite?"

Eva's lips flattened, like Jubilee had one-upped her or something. She had meant it as a curiosity question, but maybe she was pointing out that Eva was taking money out of Lana's pocket as well.

"She just finished it last year. I don't think she had it rented out solid. I'm not even sure she had it rented more than a few weeks."

"I see."

Jubilee didn't want to fight with her and wasn't trying to ruin anything for her, either. It had started out as a true question that she was just curious about.

By the time she had made two trips down to the basement to help Eva with her things and finished cleaning up the kitchen, the zucchini bread was out on the counter and cooling. With Eva down in the basement unpacking, the tension in the kitchen magically disappeared.

"Are you sure you don't mind delivering the zucchini bread?" Lana said as they wrapped the chocolate zucchini bread in order for Jubilee to transport it. Her girls were upstairs changing into their swimming things. It was going to take Jubilee a little bit of time to get used to the idea that there was a lake within walking distance and they could take a break anytime during the day to run down to take a swim. It was such a fun idea, and she loved that her kids would grow up having such a fun thing all summer long.

"I don't mind at all. In fact, I really appreciate you letting me. I want to get to know the neighbors. You know how small towns are. Everyone knows everyone else, and the sooner I start figuring out who people are and where they live, the better."

Her girls came down, and Lana helped them grab some towels from the laundry room, which she provided as a courtesy to her guests, and then she walked out the front porch with them and told them how to find Kim and Davis and their home. It wasn't hard. They walked to the end of the road, turned left, and walked a little more.

For some reason as Lana was standing there and Jubilee was listening to her instructions, she thought about asking where Matt lived.

She wasn't quite sure why that question came into her head, but she tried to push it aside. Matt shouldn't mean anything to her. All he'd done was help her when she needed it, brought her to his mom, where he knew she would have a soft landing.

She wanted to read more into that than what she knew was actually there.

Not to mention, she had the memories of him during that summer that she spent in Strawberry Sands. He wasn't the only thing she had admired that summer, but he did figure prominently in her memories.

Funny, because he didn't even know it.

She and her girls started down the street, one of them carrying a small container of drinks and snacks that Lana had packed and insisted on sending with them, and the other one carrying the beach bag full of towels and some sand toys that Lana had dug up that other guests had used.

Jubilee carried two loaves of chocolate zucchini bread.

It smelled delicious, and Lana had promised them that they would have a snack of chocolate zucchini bread when they got back from swimming.

"Mom?" Scarlett asked as they walked down the street in front of several buildings that were shuttered up, along with the diner, where a man with tattoos and two earrings in one ear was standing behind the counter chatting with a customer sitting on a stool, and another shop that looked like it might have been a surf shop at one time but was boarded up now.

"Yeah?" she said, looking down at Scarlett whose eyes were bright and eager.

"Can we live here forever?"

They hadn't even made it to the beach yet, and her daughter was in love with the quaint little town.

"What makes you ask that?" she said, instead of answering. She'd love to say yes, of course they could live there forever. But they'd hit town at the right time, June, as people were gearing up for the short tourist season. They might not have a job come winter.

"Lana is like a grandmother. I mean, like the grandmother I wish I had." Scarlett's voice kind of trailed off, like she thought maybe she shouldn't have said what she did.

"I'll ask her to be ours. I bet she'll say yes. She likes us," Penelope piped up from the other side of Jubilee.

How different this was from Cody's mom, Shirley. Shirley always had sharp words for the girls and acted like they were in the way. Pretty much two seconds after they set foot in her house, she had the TV on and acted like she didn't want them to move from in front of it.

She protected her furniture, her house, and anything that the girls might break or get dirty, like it was museum quality.

Jubilee couldn't think of anything that her girls had ever broken at Shirley's house, and she had always taken care to make sure that they were spotlessly clean when they visited. And even more so when they lived there.

She wouldn't have moved in if she had anywhere else to go. But her parents had broken up when she was small, and she'd been raised by an elderly aunt. That aunt had long since died, taking the only family that Jubilee ever really had with her.

That was in the past. It was just hard to believe that all the good things that were happening to her in Strawberry Sands were real. Or that they would continue.

Especially with Eva coming into the picture. She wasn't sure what to make of that.

She chatted with her girls as they headed to Davis and Kim's house. She didn't have to worry about knocking on the door since they were sitting out on their deck, their baby under an umbrella, both of them facing the lake.

"Hello!" Jubilee called, stepping around the house and walking up the steps to the deck.

"Hey!" Kim said, standing up. She walked forward with her hand out. "I'm Kim. And you must be Jubilee. Lana texted me and let me know that you were coming."

"She's the sweetest. Always so thoughtful," Jubilee said, appreciating how Lana had taken her under her wing and was helping her get acclimated to the town.

"Well, we've been looking forward to you coming, because she said you were bringing chocolate zucchini bread, which is like chocolate cake, only better." She glanced at Davis. "That's my husband, Davis."

"Good to meet you," Jubilee said. She turned back to Kim. "These are my girls, Scarlett and Penelope."

"It's good to meet you, girls," Kim said with a smile.

Her girls politely greeted Kim, and she chatted with them just a little.

"Is that your baby?" Penelope finally asked, peering into the little bassinet that sat under an umbrella.

"It sure is. She's sleeping right now, but I'm sure if your mom brings you back to visit, at some point she'll be awake and you can hold her if you'd like."

Penelope, for once at a loss for words, nodded her head eagerly.

Jubilee smiled. Penelope always loved playing with her dolls and babies and pretending to be a mom. Scarlett did too, but Penelope had always been so much more into it than Scarlett.

Still, they both leaned over and looked in awe at the sleeping little one.

"It looks like she's doing well," Jubilee said.

"She is. I was a little concerned. After two months in the NICU, I wasn't sure whether I was up to taking care of her at home with no nurses, but Davis is almost just as good as a nurse." She grinned over at her husband, who laughed at her.

"I was born to be a nurse, what can I say," he said easily.

They shared a look that was sweet and tender and made Jubilee smile.

"I'm sure Lana told you that we're having a bit of a celebration here next Saturday, but just in case you didn't know, I want to make sure that you know you're invited."

"She did mention it," Jubilee said, remembering that Lana had said something to the effect yesterday while they had been eating. But she talked about a bunch of different things, and it was hard to keep everything straight.

"Next Saturday. Right here. Everybody's bringing something to eat or drink, and we're providing silverware and tables and some beach chairs. Just something small to celebrate Kathleen coming home and also the fact that we got married yesterday."

"My goodness. Congratulations. I'm sure Lana mentioned it, but there were so many different people and names I just couldn't keep track of everything."

"Yeah. That's fine. Hopefully we'll get to know each other really well this summer. Are you planning on staying?"

"I'd like to. I understand that it's not always very busy in the off-season, and I don't know if I'll have a job."

"Well, that's a thought. Blueberry Beach has really grown and is starting to spill over here. So if you can just hang on by your fingernails for a little bit, there might be more."

"I'm pretty good at hanging on by my fingernails," Jubilee said with a laugh. That was true. She'd scratched her way into a lot of different places and held on tight. Maybe for longer than she should have. She thought of her marriage and the little hints that she had that her husband either wasn't faithful or was going to be unfaithful. She probably should have taken those hints, instead of ignoring them. But it was too late now, and there was no point in her beating herself up over it.

They chatted a little more, when the sound of a truck motor interrupted them.

"That's Matt bringing a load of hay. Are you okay here?" Davis said, standing and looking over toward the stable where the horses grazed up on the hill at the sparse grass that grew on the sand dunes. There was pasture out back which looked green and lush, but Jubilee could imagine that it would take a lot of hay to see the horses through the winter.

"I'm just fine. You go on," Kim said, waving him off.

"We're going to head out too. The girls and I are going to play in the lake for a little bit before we go back in and get back to work at the bed-and-breakfast."

"All right. Have a good time. And if you guys would like, you're always welcome to come and take the horses for a ride.

As long as we don't have them rented out to someone else."

"Wow. That's very generous of you. I... I rode a little bit and took lessons for about a year when I was younger. I haven't ridden in a decade or more."

"It comes back to you, like riding a bi-cycle. Our horses are very gentle. Matt has some, but they're a little bit more high-strung."

"We definitely want to start out with yours. The girls have never ridden."

"Could we do it, Mom? I really want to ride horses," Penelope begged.

"Mom? Could we?" Scarlett echoed.

"Probably not this week. We need to get settled in. But maybe next?" She lifted her brows at Kim. They were probably busy getting ready for the party on Saturday and wouldn't have time anyway. She didn't have a clue as to how to saddle up a horse or anything. She had learned it all when she'd taken lessons, but it seemed like so long ago, she couldn't even begin to remember.

Kim nodded in agreement.

She nodded back, then looked down at her girls. "We'll get together with Miss Kim, and we'll figure something out." Maybe she could talk to Lana who might have some ideas of where she could go to brush up on the things that she needed to know.

She said goodbye to Kim and tried not to take any extra glances over at Matt who had driven his truck up to the barn and backed in. It was okay to admire a man like that, she told herself, but he would never see anything of interest in her, and she would be better off if she didn't get her hopes up.

Plus, she was here for a new start. Not a new relationship. It would be best if she remembered that.

Chapter 7

"So Jubilee said she was staying with your mom," Davis said casually as he threw a hay bale off the wagon.

Matt admired Davis. He'd moved to Strawberry Sands not long ago and had been a solid support to Kim as she had their baby early and had spent a lot of time in the NICU. Matt admired the way Davis had totally been there for her, helping in any way he could and keeping the townspeople informed.

He had been thrilled to hear that they had gotten married, and while parties weren't necessarily his thing, he was looking forward to Kim and Davis's party, just because he felt like they definitely had something to celebrate. The health of their baby, their marriage, and the fact that they had finally come together as a family.

That was never going to happen with him and Eva. That ship had sailed long, long ago, if it was ever in the harbor to begin with, which he doubted. At the very most, he would hope to be able to be civil to her for the sake of their daughter.

For some reason as he was thinking that, Jubilee's face shimmered across his brain again, like it had quite often since he'd met her along the road.

"Yeah. Mom gave her a room, and her kids too. She's going to be helping her for the summer. Probably longer if I know my mom."

"I've heard she always seems to take vagabonds under her wing."

"Anyone who needs it."

"You know the world needs more people like her," Davis said casually.

"She's one of a kind, that's for sure." Although, he saw characteristics of his mom in Jubilee. Jubilee had just had things a little harder, a little earlier. His mom had her husband walk out on her after she already had six kids and a farm to run. Jubilee's circumstances might have been a little bit different, and he was curious to know her story, but he could see the compassion and caring in Jubilee that was easy to see in his mom.

"So how did Jubilee land on her doorstep again?" Davis asked, making Matt's head jerk up. Did he know the story and just wanted to rub it in?

But Davis was concentrating on throwing hay bales down and didn't have so much as a smirk on his face.

"She broke down on the road. I came across her, saw her kids, heard her story about looking for work in Strawberry Sands, and my mom seemed like a natural place to put her."

That was most of it. Although, he had to admit that if there hadn't been something about Jubilee that tugged at his heart, he might not have suggested giving her a place at his mom's.

He might have put her up at a hotel himself. Or warned her away, considering that there wasn't much work in town anyway.

Eva crossed his mind again, and he wondered how long she would last in town. Knowing his mom the way he did, she probably offered to let Eva stay for free. After all, Eva was the mother of her granddaughter whom she adored. His mom had always been way too nice to her as far as Matt was concerned. Eva just took advantage of her.

Anytime he pointed that out to his mom, she just smiled and said that God had it, and she wasn't worried about people taking advantage of her. God would reward her and even things out eventually. She had so much confidence in that fact, it was hard for Matt not to have confidence in it as well.

"You know, sometimes God puts those things in your path because He has a plan for them." Davis's words were very casual, and Matt tried not to read more into them than what was there. Davis couldn't possibly know that he'd been thinking way more about Jubilee than he should have been. Not to mention, if God had something in mind for him, it was kind of odd that God would also have Eva moving back to Strawberry Sands, even if only for a summer.

He wasn't sure whether he had read everything right that morning or not. Whether Eva really did seem like she was interested in getting together with him.

He couldn't even say "back" together, because they had never really been together.

They went on to talk about the weather and how much hay Matt was making, and that type of thing.

Matt noticed that the small girl Davis had hired shortly after Kathleen was born slipped in and out, taking care of the horses. The boy that had been with her at times was nowhere to be seen. But Matt didn't go around looking for them, although he wanted to ask about them again, because even now, the girl looked young to him.

And a little bit...haunted. He wasn't sure that was the right word, but she just seemed like someone who maybe didn't have the best homelife. He wasn't sure exactly what gave him that idea and couldn't quite put his finger on why he thought that.

But she slipped out of sight, and he forgot about her by the time they had the hay unloaded, Davis had written him out a check, and he walked out to his pickup, stopping to look over the lake.

He probably shouldn't have, because he could see Jubilee down below, playing in the sand next to the water with her daughters.

As an adult, he would have thought that she would be sitting, possibly reading a book while her girls played around her. But she chased them through the waves, laughing and splashing, and from the way she was acting, he would have thought that she wasn't much older than they were.

He smiled to watch it.

It wasn't exactly the sultry, sexy beach babe that might have caught his eye ten years ago. Eva, for example.

Jubilee wore a long skirt that flowed and waved in the breeze, whipping out behind her, patterned in bright blue and looking cheerful. Her white tunic shirt flapped along with her movements and was most definitely more than modest.

Yeah, she wouldn't have turned his head when he was a teenager, but she caught his eye now. Maybe he was older and wiser and knew that the perfect beach bod didn't necessarily mean that there was a personality that he wanted to hang around for any length of time with behind it.

But he loved the unaffected way Jubilee played with her girls. Like she didn't care whether anyone was watching and didn't expect them to.

He really didn't plan it that way, but before he thought about it, his feet were taking him down through the dunes and out onto the beach.

He stopped at the edge to take his boots and socks off and roll up his pant legs. His white legs sticking out from his jeans looked ridiculous, and he realized despite the fact that he lived next to Lake Michigan, he hadn't been in the lake at all that year.

He had no intention of swimming in his jeans, but he definitely had the intention of going down and… He wasn't sure. He was just drawn to the laughter and happiness and fun.

He should have brought Nora with him. But she'd wanted to take a nap, and he hadn't insisted, knowing that they had gotten up early in order to make the long drive to his house.

He was almost to the water when he realized he didn't have anything to say. He was just following the laughter and the fun. Was his life really that sad?

He was considering whether or not he would be able to leave without being spotted, when one of the girls splashed Jubilee, and she laughed, dragging her foot through the shallow water of the last wave and splashing her daughter back, before turning and running and plowing straight into him.

He wasn't expecting that. He might have been able to keep his feet, but the sand was uneven and he stepped into a depression as he backed up trying to keep his balance.

He ended up falling flat on his back, with Jubilee on top of him.

Not what he had planned.

Her hair was down, and it draped all over his face as her legs tangled with his and her laughter carried on the breeze.

"Oh, my goodness!" she said, trying to untangle herself from him. It was probably made harder because he somehow got his hands wrapped around her, and his brain hadn't quite gotten the message to his fingers to let her go yet.

"I'm so sorry!" she said, somehow grabbing her hair and slipping all of it back over her shoulder.

That's when she realized who she was lying on top of. He could see the second that she figured it out, as recognition entered her eyes.

"Matt?" she asked, her brows going up, her eyes widening.

"Mom! You're not supposed to plow into strange men!"

"It's okay. It's not a strange man," Jubilee said cheerfully.

He huffed out a laugh at that. "Just because I'm not a strange man doesn't mean it's okay to plow into me."

"That's what I was saying."

"Mr. Matt?" Penelope came over, wrinkling her nose, like she couldn't quite figure out what he was doing on the beach, lying down, with her mother on top of him.

"Are you okay?" Jubilee said, and he finally got his hands to let her go. But after pushing up a bit, she looked at him like she wasn't quite sure whether she might have hurt him.

"I'm fine. Just a little embarrassed. I should have caught you, not fallen with you. The only thing that would have made it worse would have been if I had fallen on top of you."

"Kind of hard to do considering that I was the one plowing into you," Jubilee said, and her voice lost none of its cheerful happiness.

He couldn't believe the difference in her from yesterday to today. He had to comment on it. "Good to see you smiling."

Her face froze for just an instant, and then she seemed to shrug. "You know, thank you so much for taking me to your mom. She has a way of making me feel like she really cares about me. And... I guess I feel like everything's going to be okay. Not necessarily because of anything she's done or said, just because... I guess I was praying last night and told the Lord that so far He's taken complete and total care of me, and it's silly for me to get upset. Isn't it?"

She said that last question a little bit more softly, just as though she had been thinking about it and was asking herself rather than him.

"I think you probably said it better than anyone else could. God is in control, and as long as we work hard and try to watch and do what He wants us to, there really isn't too much that can bother us."

Her smile stretched big again.

"Plus, look at this sky," she said, leaning to her side, looking up at the blue sky with white puffy clouds blowing in off the lake. "And the lake. It's cold and refreshing and... I just can't believe that I'm living beside it. That my girls will be here all summer long. We can go swimming whenever we want to. Is this not the most awesome thing ever?" She smiled, her lips pulling up in a huge grin, like God had given her the biggest gift in the world by letting her live beside the lake.

Matt felt a little bit guilty, because he took it for granted that he was there. It was just a part of his life, and while he loved it and enjoyed his ride every morning, he knew it didn't make him happy the way Jubilee was happy now.

"I was talking to Davis and Kim, and they said we could ride their horses along the lakeshore sometime. That just seems so...amazing."

"It is amazing. You'll have to go with me sometime."

"You ride along the beach still?" Jubilee asked as she finished untangling herself and ungracefully shoved herself to her feet, careful not to step on her skirt. She reached out a hand for him.

He took it, then tried to gather himself so he wasn't pulling on her too hard as he stood up. "Every morning. Even in winter. Unless it's dangerously cold for the horses. I just bundle up, and we go. It's fun to see the different ways the lake looks every day. It's never the same."

"I guess it takes a sharp eye to notice that. Someone who's seen it every day of their life. Because, to me, it looks ex-actly the same as it did fifteen years ago when I was a kid and sat on the beach, dreaming about what my life would be like."

Chapter 8

Jubilee and Matt stood, and maybe they should have been looking at the lake, but they ended up facing each other.

He looked down at her, windblown, sand on her face and in her hair, her clothes all flapping in the wind, but a big smile on her face and dreams in her eyes.

Whatever she'd been through, it hadn't beaten her. The cheating husband, a divorce, two girls who depended on her, and not even enough money for gas in her gas tank, and here she was, finding things to be thankful for, talking about God like He was right beside her, and convicting Matt of not appreciating all the things in his life, because she was so happy with so little.

He had a house, his mom and siblings all lived close, and he could lean on them anytime he needed them. He had a thriving business and horses he could ride every morning. He had the summer to look forward to with his daughter and enough money that he wasn't worried about feeding her.

He didn't like the guilty feeling, but he appreciated the fact that she inspired him to want to be better. Saying a little prayer of thanks, which he vowed to expound upon later, he said, "Maybe you're right. Maybe since I see it every day, I notice every little thing that changes. Or maybe I just want to see the change. And I like thinking about the fact that it's never the same. Because you're right. It's still blue like it always used to be."

She laughed. "I guess I'm not that observant. It just looks pretty to me. And I'm always amazed at the size and the vastness. It's just a lake, but you can't even see the other side."

"Yeah. It's really big. You can drive up the shore for hours and not come to the end. I guess I don't think about that nearly as often as what I should." He couldn't tell her how she'd already convicted him just by the little bit that she was saying.

"What are you doing down here? Did you want to go swimming?"

"Don't be silly, Penelope. He's wearing jeans. Of course he's not going swimming."

"Well, I have gone swimming in jeans, but I wasn't planning on it today. I just saw you guys down here, and I thought it would be fun to come down and see how you were doing."

He ended lamely, because he knew that wasn't a very good reason to go down. Just to check on them? What was he, like her dad or something?

He could hardly say you guys looked like you were having so much fun I felt drawn to you and was down here before I thought about it. That sounded just as stupid.

He didn't really want to leave them, and Jubilee didn't look like she was in a big rush to run off either. He racked his brain for something to say and pulled out the first thing he could.

"Are you going to Kim and Davis's party?"

"Kim just mentioned it. Yeah. I would like to get involved in the community. And that seems like a good way. I'll probably talk to your mom, because Kim said something about everybody bringing something. And I really have no idea.

Not to mention, I don't exactly have a kitchen."

"I can tell you that my mom doesn't care if you use hers. She loves having people around. I think that she would have been very happy if all of her kids had stayed in that house with her and never moved out."

"That sounds like a mom. I...didn't have one."

"You had to come from someone," he said and then wished he wouldn't have, because he understood what she meant. And he hadn't been very considerate.

But she smiled and didn't look especially sad. "No. I guess my mom just ran off when I was a baby, and my dad gave me to my Aunt Teresa. He's alive somewhere, but I only heard from him a couple of times in my childhood, and when Aunt Teresa died, he didn't even come to the funeral."

"I don't even understand how someone could be like that. It makes me sad. I have such a great family."

"I love your mom. She's just so...maternal. Like I just feel like I'm so welcome and loved every time I'm with her. I hope that's true."

"Trust me, it is. She loves taking in strays and anyone who looks like they need her. I was just thinking that you have a lot of her traits. You remind me of her."

"I do?" Jubilee didn't look like she believed him at all.

"You do. Truly. This is the kind of thing that my mom would do. Playing in the waves with her kids and never caring who watched. I... After Dad left, I always wished she would get married again. Not to have more children, but just because she has so much love, and from what I could see, she was such a great wife. After Dad left, he was only gone about four months when he asked to come back. She had the locks changed, and she wouldn't let him in. But it just kind of made me think that he realized what he had after he left."

"It's too bad he couldn't have realized that before."

Her kids had gone to play, but he barely registered their squealing and splashing. Jubilee's face shone, but it was more than just her happiness that spoke to him. He'd enjoyed talking to her the day before too.

"I think sometimes as humans, we don't really realize what we have until it's gone. Maybe it's hard for us to imagine life without it. Or..."

"Or it's the grass is always greener on the other side of the fence thing."

"Exactly. We don't realize what a lie that is until we're actually on the other side of the fence and see that there are places of good grass there, but it is the same or worse than what we already had."

He had seen that more than once with his horses, where they tried to push through the fence to get out to get a couple of tufts of grass that weren't worth much. He liked to think that he was smarter than a horse, but maybe he wasn't.

Although, he had never left where he was, thinking that he was going some-where better.

But he supposed in normal circum-stances, he might have had a tendency to just stand back and let things happen with Jubilee. Something told him that this was the time that he needed to step forward and pursue what he wanted.

Not looking for greener grass, but mak-ing sure that he didn't lose the best thing that could have ever happened to him.

Odd thoughts, since he barely knew her. But she brought out the good in him.

She made him admire her, she laughed and...made him want to run down to the beach and put his feet in the lake.

"All right. I suppose I ought to get back to work. This was a nice break though. I'm glad you guys were down here laughing and having a good time. I would be in the truck heading back to my farm if you hadn't been. And I would have missed this. This reminder about how beautiful everything is and how much I should appreciate it."

"You would have also missed me plowing you over, which probably would be a good thing. You might be feeling that tomorrow."

"I'm sure I will. I'm a little older than I used to be."

"It happens to everyone, doesn't it?"

"It does." He hadn't made any move to leave, neither had she, and he stared into her eyes now. Thinking about getting older. Thinking about chances and taking them, even when they seemed scary.

"You want to go with me to the party on Saturday?"

He held his breath. How long had it been since he asked anyone out? Years. And he hadn't meant to do it just now. But he didn't regret it, and he also didn't think he did too bad. She didn't look shocked or surprised or horrified.

"You know I come with two girls." She sighed and looked away, toward the lake where they played, before she looked back at him. "And a whole lot of baggage. You might not want to go with me."

"And why wouldn't I? I hadn't smiled this much in...years. And that is no exaggeration."

"Well, you make a soft landing anyway." She laughed and shrugged her shoulders.

"I think that was an insult. I'm pretty sure I'm supposed to be hard, a wall of cement. Pure, solid muscle."

"All right. It was the sand. The sand makes a soft landing. Underneath the pure, solid muscle."

She was teasing him, and he had to laugh.

"All right. I'll probably see you before Saturday, in fact..." He opened his mouth, hardly daring to believe the words were coming out. "I usually take a ride at sunrise along the lake. You want to come with me tomorrow?"

"I'd love to." She didn't hesitate.

And then he remembered. Nora was there. He and Nora always took sunrise rides.

"Uh... I forgot. Nora is here. She'll want to go."

"All right. Never mind." She shrugged her shoulders like it didn't matter. "You come with a daughter too. I just come with double that."

She understood. He appreciated that he'd messed up and asked her to do something he couldn't follow through on, and she was totally cool with it.

"How about a sunset ride?" he asked. He was more likely to have his horses rented out at sunset and sunrise, but he had two available tonight. "Tonight?"

"All right. I'm helping your mom, but I'm pretty sure she's not going to tell me I can't go for a ride, if we go back down and I work until almost dark."

"My mom's not a slave driver. She'll actually be happy to see me going with someone. And unless I miss my guess, she'll be thrilled it's you."

"If you say so. You should know better than me." She shrugged her shoulders like she wasn't sure whether that was actually true or not. Like she couldn't believe that his mom would actually want him to be with her. He could assure her that that was the case, but he didn't.

"All right. I'll be there to pick you up. You don't need to worry about wearing anything special or...getting dressed up or anything."

"In other words, I can work until it's time to go?" she said with a laugh.

He nodded, surprised that she understood what he was trying to say, even though he didn't say it in such a great way. "Yeah. That."

They stared at each other for just a bit more before he started to walk away. Smiling. Waving a bit before he turned fully toward the dunes and strode toward his boots and socks.

He just met her yesterday, but he had such a great time when he was around her. He almost felt like he was a teenager, where he wanted to spend every waking second with her. Was that crazy?

Chapter 9

Rodney held himself very still and pretended to be asleep.

The scratching on the window had gotten to be very familiar over the last eight weeks. Pretty soon the door slid open, slowly and quietly, and then a soft footstep, another, and the door slid shut.

He smiled to himself. He'd taken to leaving a pillow and a blanket on the comfortable chair that sat in the corner of his room.

Becky typically slipped in, and the first couple times, he caught her lying on the floor.

Then, once he removed all of the dirty clothes, school papers, and a basketball that had been covering the chair, she started lying on it. Then, he got a little smarter and thought about setting out the blanket and pillow.

She still hadn't told him where she came from or what she did. Where she went.

But he felt like she was trusting him more. Even though he couldn't go help her every day. His parents expected him to do all the things that a kid from a family like theirs did. Golfing, going out in the sailboat on the lake, whether with their friends or with his dad.

He had his summer pretty much scheduled.

But he'd gotten off when he could.

His bed sagged, and his eyes flew open.

This was new.

He held his breath. He realized now it was raining outside, and he could hear teeth chattering as Becky leaned over, her other leg coming up silently.

He hadn't even considered the rain. Despite the summer day, or night rather, it was chilly.

He should have slid over more, but it was too late now. If he did that, she'd know he was awake.

Carefully, she slowly moved down until she was lying beside him. Her back to his front. Thankfully, he was under the covers, and he'd taken to wearing a pair of sweatpants to bed. He hadn't put on a T-shirt, but he determined that from then on, he would.

This was not a good thing. He could be in serious trouble if he got caught like this. But her shivering teeth got to him.

She must have grabbed the blanket from the chair, because she pulled it over top of herself and curled up in a ball, touching him for the warmth he could give.

He supposed, if he was in for a penny, he should be in for the whole pound.

His arm came out and went around her.

"Be still. You're freezing," he said softly, his chin at the top of her head as he tucked her closer to him.

She must have been extremely cold, because she didn't protest. It was very seldom that Becky didn't protest about something. It seemed to be her nature to never accept anything at face value. To always question.

Maybe it was just her upbringing or the way she'd been raised.

"I'm sorry. I didn't mean to wake you up." Her words came out between the clacking of her jaw, pinched, like she was pulling herself as tight inside as she could, to conserve heat.

"You didn't wake me. You never do. I'm always up, listening."

She stiffened, if that were possible, and he pulled her closer, willing her to get warm. He didn't want her to catch pneumonia.

"You sneak," she hissed, her teeth not clacking quite as much as they had been.

"That's you. You're the one that's sneaking into my bedroom. Do you know how much trouble I would be in if anyone caught you?"

"I always leave as soon as the sun comes up. Sometimes before." Her words were still hissed, but the anger wasn't in them anymore.

"I know. Tell me why," he finally said at last, after she paused, hoping that he wasn't pushing her and she wouldn't jump out of the bed and run off into the rain. That was the last, very last, thing he wanted.

She was quiet for a while, though her teeth still chattered, and he knew she wasn't asleep. Her hair was wet, and it soaked into his pillow, making his chin and neck wet with big, cold drops that clung to him. It only emphasized how cold she must be.

Summer in Michigan could get hot, but the nights often chilled down no matter how hot the days were. Especially with the breeze off the lake.

"You can't tell anyone. Promise?"

"Promise," he said casually.

"Swear on your life that you won't breathe a word of it to anyone."

He smiled at her drama. It couldn't be that bad. Maybe she just enjoyed sneaking out of the house.

Maybe her dad came home drunk. That wasn't quite as funny, but he'd never seen any bruises or anything else on her. So he knew she wasn't being beaten or someone was very careful to put the bruises where a normal person wouldn't see them.

"I swear. You're awful demanding considering that you crawled into my bed in the middle of the night, and I really should kick you out. You're worse than a little sister, Beckpet."

"Shut up, Dixie," she said, but there was no heat in her words.

She snuggled down a little more, and he tucked the blanket more securely around her, pulling her closer to his chest. He hardly thought if he had a sister he would hold her like this, but there was nothing romantic about it. He was affectionate toward her because he admired her pluck and her scrappiness. Nothing else.

Still, no one would understand that if anyone saw them. And she wouldn't be the one in trouble. Even though she was the one who kept sneaking into his room, and he was the one who was too kindhearted to send her away. He tried not to hold her too tight because he wanted to know why.

"My little sister is with foster parents just outside of Strawberry Sands. I visit her and make sure that she's getting everything that she needs."

"So why don't you just go back to your house when you're done? Why do you come here?"

She was quiet for a minute, and then she said, "They took my sister out of the foster home that we shared because these people said they wanted to adopt her. They didn't want me, because, well, you know. How I am. And they didn't want two girls, either. Anyway, I ran away."

She said the last part just as casually as she could, like she couldn't shock him more if she would have socked him in the stomach.

"You ran away." He tried to say that as casually as she did, although he suspected he did not succeed.

"Yeah. How else was I going to see my sister?"

"So you're hanging out outside of your sister's house?"

"And here."

"So the day that you were here was the first day that your sister moved into her new house?" He hoped that was true. He couldn't imagine Becky running around in a Michigan winter. She could have died. She probably would have.

"Yeah, well, it was like the fourth or fifth day. I needed to get something to eat."

Holy cow.

It was worse than he thought. Becky was...homeless.

"Is anyone looking for you?"

"Probably. Maybe my face is on the wall in Walmart."

"That's great. They'll find you in my room, you'll be in trouble, and then I'll have charges brought against me for kidnapping."

"Relax, Dixie. I'll tell them you didn't do it."

"That's not good enough."

It might help him, but he would still be in big, big trouble.

Still, he couldn't just not do anything. Becky was far worse off than what he thought. She didn't have a home. No wonder she slipped into his room at night. At least he'd gotten her a job.

"You're buying food for yourself, right?"

"Sometimes."

"What do you mean sometimes?"

"There's no grocery store in Strawberry Sands." He could feel her thin little shoulder shrugging. "And I can't hardly go to the diner and eat every day. They're going to ask a whole pile of questions."

Of course. Of course. He liked to think he was suave and sophisticated, maybe not exactly a man of the world, but becoming that. But this little street urchin, this little homeless girl, had far more common sense and street smarts than he did. Of course she couldn't go to the diner every day. Someone was bound to notice and call some kind of authorities. Not to mention, in a town like Strawberry Sands, everybody knew everything about everyone else.

"I should call the authorities on you."

"You promised!" She struggled to sit up.

"Calm down, Beckpet," he said, pulling her back against him. At least if she were mad, she'd get warm faster. Her teeth were hardly chattering at all now.

Of course, she probably carried a knife and she wouldn't hesitate to slit his throat if she thought she needed to. He was under no illusions that Becky wouldn't do whatever it took to get what she wanted. She was scrappy. He smiled a little. She reminded him of a mangy, scrounging stray dog or, more like it, a cat who wasn't afraid to fight for what it wanted.

She was definitely not a puppy dog.

But really, he should call someone. The kid couldn't run around without a home. Without a family. Without parents. But it made sense to him now. Becky was anything if not fiercely loyal, and he could see her running away just so that she wouldn't be separated from the one bit of family she had.

Made him a little bit sad to think about it. Partly because he didn't have anyone to be that loyal to, and partly because family shouldn't be separated.

"Where are your parents?"

"Don't know." Her words were simple, but they were a little bit too studiously casual for him to believe that the answer was quite that easy.

"Don't know? You don't want to tell me?"

"You're a big fat nosy brat, Dixie," she spit out, but her words didn't sound like an attack, they were just...her spouting off.

"All right. Does that make you feel better? Now tell me where they are."

"I don't know where my dad is. And my mom is in prison, and I'll be an adult with kids of my own before she gets out. So forget that. There's no one to rescue me. No daddy to take me home to. And if you're going to try, I'm leaving."

He was older she was, but she acted like the adult. And he believed her mom probably was in jail. She probably raised her little sister until they'd gotten put in foster care.

He had a whole bunch of questions he wanted to ask, but he figured he knew enough for now.

"All right. Here's what we're going to do. I'll have food in my room from now on."

"I'm not taking your charity, Dixie."

"Calm down, Beckpet. I'm gonna charge you for it. You can let the money sit on my dresser. I'll make sure you have plenty to eat." He thought about it. He needed to get her clothes too. She needed a raincoat, sweatshirt, something. Come to think of it, she'd shown up in the same red shirt every time he'd seen her. It was nondescript, and he hadn't really paid attention.

"Is that the only outfit you have?"

"What of it, Dixie?"

She really did remind him of a cat with its back up, claws out and hissing.

"People are bound to notice that you never change your clothes. Someone's going to figure out what's going on."

"You're just saying that, because you're planning to tell someone, then you're gonna tell me that people figured it out on their own. I'm not stupid. I knew I shouldn't trust you." She tried to get up again, but he didn't allow her to push his arm off.

"Beckpet, calm down. Let me think. We need to get you some clothes so that people don't figure out that you're not changing. It's not normal for a girl to wear the same outfit all the time. I can probably get you some T-shirts." He might have a few things stuffed in the back of his closet that were too small for him. "But I can't get you pants. No one's going to believe that I need girl pants for anything."

"I don't have to wear girl pants, genius. They're the same as boy pants anyway."

He didn't think so, but he didn't argue with her. "I could probably get you shorts. I don't know. When I get my driver's license, I can go to the store without asking and buy whatever I want to."

"I'm not taking your charity," she said again, although her voice had started to sound sleepy. She must be getting warm.

"I'll charge for them too. I'll leave the price tags on so you know exactly how much you owe me."

It wasn't like he needed the money. He'd keep it somewhere and make sure she got it back. He wasn't charging the homeless girl for food and clothes. That was ridiculous. But Becky could be as stubborn as the day was long. After all, it was eight long weeks that he'd known her before she finally confessed that she didn't have a home.

No stinking home.

He couldn't believe it. Couldn't believe she'd been homeless and hadn't breathed a word of it. Well, he kind of did. Becky was the kind of kid who would be desperate to stay with her sister. That was who she was. How could he not admire that? How could he not want to help her?

There had to be some way to figure things out. Something he could do.

Her breathing had evened out, and her body had relaxed under his arm. She fell asleep.

That was just as well. He adjusted her some, trying to move her head to a more dry spot on his pillow.

The central air was on at his house. If he were able, he'd turn it off. She didn't need that cold air blowing on her as wet and cold as she was.

He shook his head, careful not to wake her. He couldn't believe she was homeless.

Then he smiled. He loved that she would go to such lengths to keep her little "family" together. The world needed more people like her, not less. More people who would fight for their families. Fight for their relationships. Fight for the things that matter. Stop fighting stuff that didn't.

Kind of funny when he thought about how a little kid, smart-mouthed and sassy, stubborn and irritating, could remind him about the important things of life.

He hoped he never forgot.

Chapter 10

"How do I look?" Chi said, smoothing her hair down, then brushing her hands down her shirt.

"Like you've been working since five this morning," Griff said calmly, not even glancing up at her. More irritated than he wanted to admit that she was preening for that stupid big-city lawyer.

"Really?" she asked, and his heart twisted at the dismay in her voice. He wanted to encourage her, not discourage her.

But she couldn't see that the lawyer was nothing but a cheat. He had a light, a very light, ring on the third finger on his left hand. Griff had noticed it the last time he was in, when he'd been holding his coffee cup. It wouldn't surprise Griff at all if the man took his wedding band off before he walked into the diner.

Why else would he come the whole way to Strawberry Sands for coffee unless he was trolling for women? Griff probably knew more about that than he wanted to admit. Still, it irritated him that Chi wasn't smart enough to figure it out.

"Do you think I'm pretty?" she asked softly, leaning forward like his answer really mattered.

He thought she was beautiful. Beautiful because she was so fresh faced and innocent. She might think that she had a rough-and-tumble life, but she really didn't even know what that was.

Not like him.

"You're pretty," he said, but his words were given begrudgingly. He didn't want to tell her that she was pretty just so that she could go back to preening for some other man. He wanted to tell her she was pretty as he was brushing her hair back away from her cheek, tucking it behind her ear, pulling her close to himself.

That wasn't what she wanted, and if there was one thing Griff had figured out in his life, it was that he couldn't control what someone else wanted. He could only control himself. And he was limited at that. After all, he couldn't keep his eyes from drifting to her every time she walked around. Couldn't keep from watching her hands as she wrote down orders and picked up dishes. Couldn't keep from looking at the expressions that flitted across her face. Couldn't keep from wanting to help her every chance he could.

Of course, if she were successful in catching the eye of the lawyer, she'd probably close the diner and move to the big city with him.

He'd put her up somewhere, somewhere where his wife wouldn't find out about her, and she'd be his booty call.

Griff hated that. Chi was worth so much more. He supposed she'd find out a little more about the lifestyle that she thought she already was experienced in and all the pain that came with it.

She gave him a smile and said, "Wish me luck," before she turned, grabbing her tray and her notepad at the last minute, stuffing it into her pocket, smoothing her hair down one more time, and walking out.

He hated that he did it, but he picked up a rag and a tray, waited ten seconds, and then walked out behind her. Unable to just let things happen without watching out for her.

He didn't trust the fancy lawyer and didn't want Chi to be hurt.

She stood at the table of the liar, smiling and talking as he pulled his phone up and glanced down.

Her smile dimmed just a bit as his fingers flew across the screen, answering whatever text or email came in before he set it back down and looked back up at her.

When he did, it was like the sun came out from behind the clouds and shone on her face as it brightened and she glowed again.

Griff tried hard not to wish that she glowed like that for him, but he did.

And he knew that she didn't. She didn't even notice him. Or maybe she just saw the tats and the rings and dismissed him as a drifter she wouldn't be interested in.

And that was all he was. Anymore anyway. He'd left the life that he built a few years ago because it was empty and unfulfilling. Of course, he had his share of other empty and unfulfilling things as well.

Stopping here in Strawberry Sands, the sense of community, and working with Chi every day had given his life new meaning.

The bell jingled, and the little girl that had been around periodically stepped inside.

She always had a closed, serious look on her face as she walked to the corner table, her usual one, and sat down. Chi didn't even look over, too engrossed in conversation with the lawyer to pay any attention.

There were only two other tables with customers, and he'd already cooked the food for them. So he walked over and stopped at the little girl's table.

"You want your usual?" he asked, knowing that she typically got a grilled cheese sandwich, mac and cheese, and a burger. He'd never been successful in seeing her when she left, but he suspected that she didn't eat the grilled cheese right away. He wasn't sure what she did with it. Maybe she took it home to feed her dog.

He probably shouldn't care, but there was just something about her that made him think that things weren't quite what they seemed. It wasn't just because she was a little girl coming into a diner and eating by herself, either.

"Yeah. My usual," she said, and he could be mistaken, but he thought she made her voice sound a little deeper than what it naturally might be.

"Remind me of what you drink."

"I'll have a Coke."

"I'll have it right out for you."

She nodded, then looked out the window, like she didn't want to watch him, didn't want to make eye contact, didn't want him looking at her any more than what he had to.

He could read a dismissal when he saw one, and it made him even more curious. There was something going on there.

Normally he would talk to Chi about it, but she was still over at the lawyer's table. Her laughter rang out, and maybe he just wanted it to sound that way, but it seemed fake and shrill.

Not her normal belly laugh, but something she forced out to make a man feel good.

He'd been around women like that. Women who pretended to be something they weren't in order to get something they wanted. He hadn't figured Chi to be that kind of woman. Except, he thought the only thing she wanted was the lawyer. He couldn't imagine she was after his money, which probably made her even more appealing to the man.

What in the world did she see in him?

Griff wanted to stop and study him, to try to figure out what it was that attracted Chi. Was it just the fact that he gave her attention? Was it his charming smile?

It looked like he asked a question, and if possible, Chi's smile got bigger. Maybe it was because he cared about her, or at least Chi imagined that he did.

Couldn't Chi see that Griff cared about her too? Griff cared about her more. Griff cared about her in a real way, not in a my wife is at home and I'm out on the prowl and looking for an easy lay kind of way.

Griff gritted his teeth and walked into the kitchen, the little girl's order rolling in his head. He shoved thoughts of her aside and tried to figure out how he could compete with the fancy lawyer.

He could wear a suit to work. That would probably make Chi do a double take, but it would also make her laugh, he was almost sure. After all, cooks didn't come to work in a suit and tie. Even if he'd worn more than his share over his lifetime. And while he wasn't completely comfortable in one, he wore one comfortably, if that made sense.

He had the mac and cheese in the microwave and was putting the burger together when Chi walked in, a dreamy look on her face.

"He wants me to go out with him!" she said in a whisper-shout. "Can you believe it?" She sounded like a high school girl, thrilled about being asked out for her first date.

Griff slapped lettuce down, then realized he forgot the mayonnaise, took the lettuce back off, and squirted some on.

The girl asked for extra onion.

"I said, can you believe it? He asked me out. Me! He wants to take me to a fancy restaurant. Down in Blueberry Beach. There's a new one that just opened, and he said you have to wait ten days to get a reservation. He's going to make one for us tonight. In ten days, I will be going out with Mr. James Connolly, Esq." She seemed to waltz across the floor, waving the ticket that she pulled from her pad. "He wants the veggie burger, baked, not grilled, extra lettuce, no tomato, no onion, with light mayo." She said the order like it was some kind of Holy Grail. And he wanted to tell her how ridiculous it was. How ridiculous that man was.

"And he wants a side of vegetables, broccoli if we have it, with carrots. No butter. Light salt and no stems."

Did she really want to be with a man who was that picky?

Griff wanted to roll his eyes. No, what he wanted to do was grab her by the shoulders and ask her what her problem was.

"Griff. You need to hurry. I don't want to keep him waiting. I want him to come back."

"You think he's married?" Griff wanted to slap the words back into his mouth, but they were already out.

If he really loved Chi, if he loved her as much as he thought he did, he should be supporting her. If this was what she wanted, he should be helping her to get what she wanted, not resentful that she wanted someone who was so far beneath her.

"Of course he's not married. That's ridiculous. He wouldn't be asking me out if he were already married to somebody else, Griff. Not everybody lives in the slum world you came from."

That stung. But it was true.

True for half of his life anyway. Half of it, he lived on the other side, the side where the lawyer came from. That didn't live that much different than the half that he came from to begin with.

He wanted to tell Chi that. To let her know that the business world wasn't all roses and candies the way she thought it was.

That people lied. People cheated. It was a common thing. It wasn't everyone, but it was enough. Enough that a person had to be careful. Griff could see the signs, and he wanted to warn her, but the fact that he just asked a simple question and she'd gotten all defensive told him that she would ignore him if he said anything else.

She huffed away, muttering under her breath. Grabbing the coffee pot and setting a mug down on the counter and filling it. "Do I need to make his burger? I can't believe you asked such a thing. What were you trying to do, deliberately sabotage my chances? I could get out of this town. I could actually have a family with a fine man, an honorable man. Someone who has a decent job and doesn't look like he deals drugs for a living."

She was angry, obviously, and that was a slam against him. So he looked like a drug dealer to her? He couldn't change the tats. Well, he could pay to have them removed, but that didn't always work, and a lot of times, it made a person look worse than what they had before. No, they were the scars from his life before.

His earrings as well.

He had kind of hoped that Chi could see beyond that though. He shouldn't expect more from her than he expected from himself. He often judged people by the way they looked. Why shouldn't she?

He knew what he had to do, and although he hated to do it, it was right.

"I'm sorry."

He was sorry that he had upset her. Sorry that the man she wanted wasn't the man she thought he was. Sorry that she was going to get hurt. Sorry that he couldn't do anything to stop it or change it.

"I'm sorry, Griff. I got a little huffy, too. I'm sure you probably didn't mean anything by it. I know you just try to protect everyone who comes across your path." She gave a little smile. "Do you have any of that strawberry cheesecake left? You know, the one you made the other day? The one that everyone who came raved about?"

He'd saved the last piece for her. She had loved it so much yesterday that when people had asked, he told them that it was gone. Which was true, all except for one piece which he'd put back for her.

"I have one piece left." He walked to the refrigerator and pulled the plate out. He'd put plastic wrap on it with two toothpicks holding it up.

"Oh my goodness. You are the best."

He almost thought she was going to put her arms around him, but she didn't. Instead, she held them both out for the plate.

"Okay. I'm going to take this out and tell him it's on the house. Thank you." She grinned at him. "You're the best!"

She twirled on her foot, grabbed the coffee cup, and carried the cheesecake and coffee out. He pressed his lips together and went back to making the burger, flipping the grilled cheese sandwich at exactly the right moment.

He could hear the shrill laughter again, could tell that she wasn't really laughing at what he was saying, she was laughing because she thought he expected her to, and she wanted to make him happy.

Lord, why am I pining over someone who doesn't care for me and never will?

He put the top on the hamburger, stuck a toothpick in it, grabbed the grilled cheese from the griddle, set it on the plate, and cut it into diagonals.

There was no answer from the Lord. Maybe he shouldn't expect one. Of course he knew the Lord loved him, because God was love, and God loved everyone, but a man reaped what he sowed, and in his prior life, he'd sowed a lot of things that he really didn't want to have to reap.

After all, once upon a time, he'd been a lawyer just like the fancy one sitting at the table. James Connolly.

He threw the veggie patty in the oven for James, got the veggies out of the freezer, put them in the microwave, then grabbed the little girl's sandwiches and her mac and cheese and her Coke and walked back out to her table.

She was still sitting there, looking out the window. Still and quiet. Unnaturally so.

He figured it would be pointless to try to talk to Chi until the fancy lawyer left, but he made a point to try to remind himself to say something to her. There was something going on with this little girl, and they should probably try to figure it out.

Although, as he set the food down in front of her, and she thanked him for that and for the Coke, he thought that maybe he'd keep it to himself for a little bit. And just keep an eye on her.

"Where are your parents?" he asked.

"They work during the day. They leave money for me so I can go eat when I want to. It gives me a break from having SpaghettiOs at home."

"You're old enough to be by yourself?"

"My parents think so," the girl said, giving him a lifted brow.

He could read the dismissal on her face. "Can I get you anything else?"

"No thanks," she said, without looking up again.

She dug into her food, her mouth full with cheeks bulging before he walked away. Chi's laughter trailed again, and his heart squeezed, but he went back to the kitchen, determined to make her lawyer the meal he wanted, exactly the way he wanted. If anything happened between him and Chi, and Chi didn't get what she wanted, he didn't want Chi to come back on him.

He thought it was the right idea, and maybe he'd get a chance to tell that to Chi, but he wasn't going to deliberately sabotage anything. That wouldn't win him any points.

After all, he could be wrong.

Chapter 11

Jubilee walked home with her girls, smiling the whole time. She had so much fun playing in the lake with her daughters. For a little bit, she'd forgotten all about her problems. The fact that she had no money, that she wasn't sure whether she would have a job this fall and winter, that she was depending on the kindness of an almost stranger in order to house her and her girls.

Charity. She'd never depended on charity before.

Lana made it easy, easy to forget that it was charity, easy to think that she actually was being helpful and that she enjoyed the company of her girls and herself, too.

She determined that she would do as much as she could to make the bed-and-breakfast and any of the other farm businesses a success.

That was the thought in her heart as she laughed with her daughters while they walked up the main street in Strawberry Sands to the bed-and-breakfast. Lana and a woman about her age that she hadn't met, but that she would bet was one of Lana's daughters, sat on their shady front porch.

Sure enough when she walked up the walk, Lana stood and greeted her. "Jubilee! Scarlett and Penelope. You guys are smiling and look like you had a great time."

"We did!" her girls said, and then they both launched into tales of sandcastles and cold water and how they chased each other and played and how they wanted to go back again the next day.

Lana listened until they talked themselves out, and then she said, "Why don't you guys go upstairs and change out of your wet clothes, and then if it's okay with your mom, we'll have some ice cream and chocolate zucchini bread on the back porch."

The girls squealed and then looked at Jubilee, who nodded with a smile, although there was guilt in her heart. She appreciated Lana so much, but she felt like there wasn't much she could do in return, and she wanted to.

Once the girls had left, Lana said, "This is my daughter, Clara. She usually does the garden for me, but she's just been too busy this year, so it's a real godsend that you were going to take over. If you don't mind, she has time this afternoon to run out and show you what she does."

"Of course. If I can change my clothes first, I'll go right away." Jubilee took a step toward the door. "And thank you.

I... It just feels so homey and cozy here, because you've been so welcoming and kind to us. You don't have to entertain my girls if you don't want to."

"I love having them around. I wish my own grandchildren were around more. Although, hopefully once Nora gets settled in with Matt, she'll be here every day too. Typically she walks up the street to visit at least a little."

"She might be here this evening. Matt and I were going to go for a horse ride along the beach." Maybe Jubilee shouldn't have said that, since both Lana's and Clara's brows went way up at her words.

"Matt's taking you on a horse ride?" Clara said, standing up and coming over. "By the way, it's really nice to meet you." She held her hand out, which Jubilee took and shook.

"You have a wonderful mom, and you grew up in a beautiful house."

"And right beside Lake Michigan. A kid couldn't ask for more. Although, I think as children we don't always appreciate what we have. There was a lot of work involved, and sometimes I just couldn't wait to leave. Now most of the time, I wish I would never have left." She smiled and didn't look particularly unhappy, but Jubilee knew what she was saying. That a person didn't always appreciate what they had until it was gone.

"Just give me a couple minutes to change, then I'll meet you out back in the garden."

Clara nodded with a smile, and Jubilee had the feeling that she and Clara were going to be good friends.

She changed quickly, noting that her girls were laughing in their room and getting along. Sometimes it seemed like all they did was fight, but a couple of days in Strawberry Sands had them acting like friends rather than constantly bickering. She hoped it would continue. Of course, Lana was such a good influence on them too. Always cheerful and looking for something to do, someone to bless, someone to give a smile to.

Matt had said that she reminded him of his mother. She felt like she wasn't even close to being like his mother, but Lana was someone she aspired to be like eventually.

Some day.

She put her wet clothes over the back of the chair and checked her girls to make sure that they had not left theirs in a heap on the floor either. If they were going to go to the lake every day, they probably were going to be wearing the same clothes over and over again, and it would save on laundry and work if the clothes were hung up somewhere where they could dry.

She smiled when she saw that both of the girls had thrown their clothes over the foot of the bed.

They would dry just fine.

With a song in her heart and a smile on her lips, she walked down the stairs, listening to Lana in the kitchen as she talked to the girls and got them ice cream, before she cut through the sitting room and walked through the sunroom and out the back door.

The sunroom was probably her favorite room in the whole house. She could only imagine how nice it would be in the winter to be able to see the lake from inside and to enjoy the sunshine without the cold.

Would she still be here in the winter?

The thought gave her pause, but she tried to push it aside. She wasn't going to worry about it. Not today. There wasn't anything she could do, other than keep an eye out for a job that would sustain her all year. Rather, she needed to be grateful for what she had, looking for an opportunity to give back.

Somehow that seemed important. That, if God were going to bless her, she needed to turn around and see who she could bless. After all, God didn't want to give her things just so she could hoard them to herself.

The garden wasn't a typical garden. Not like Jubilee was used to seeing, with rows tilled up in the dirt, and everything on level ground. Lana's garden consisted of fifteen or twenty raised beds. They weren't wooden beds, like the kind Jubilee was used to seeing, but had some kind of metal type sides to them. They had been filled with dirt or something, and at least half of them looked as though they were planted with spring vegetables. Peas, onions, beets, radishes, and lettuce.

Jubilee gave a small prayer of thanks to her aunt who had raised her and who had had a large garden every year. At least Jubilee knew what she was looking at.

"I've never worked on raised beds before," Jubilee said as she walked toward Clara who stood beside a container full of onions.

"It makes everything so much easier. We have weed fabric down on the paths and mulch on top of it. There is no weeding anything except the dirt inside the raised beds, and I've been careful to put cardboard down before I put any kind of compost in each year. So that's kept the weeds down there. I don't know about you, but the worst part of gardening for me is weeding."

Jubilee laughed. "I know this is crazy, but I don't really mind weeding. Unless the ground is really dry and the weeds don't come out very well, and then it's frustrating."

"You are my new best friend, because I'm happy to plant, I'm happy to water, I'm happy to harvest. I'm even happy to go into the kitchen and cut and cook and can. But weeding? I hate it."

"All right then. I'll be the official weeder."

"You might be the official everything. I have a job offer that will take me to the Cities. I haven't accepted it yet. But I've been thinking about it."

"More money?" Jubilee guessed.

Clara nodded. "I've got as far as I can in my job here. If I want to advance at all, if I want to make more, I need to move."

Jubilee knew how that was. Not that she ever really experienced it. She'd gone from low-wage job to low-wage job, after marrying not long after high school. She never wanted to be a part of the corporate world, and that was part of the reason. She didn't have a thirst for advancement or for climbing the corporate ladder. She just wanted to be a mom to her kids and a wife to her husband.

"Seems to me that what your mom has right here is the perfect setup."

"You know, the longer I live, the more I think that's true. I... Maybe that's why I'm having such a hard time deciding whether or not I'm going to take this job. I don't really want to move, sure. And don't really want to be even more stuck in the grind of nine to five. I want to... I'm just not sure. Isn't that terrible?"

"No. I don't think it's terrible. I think we're probably pushed into doing things we don't want to do because that's what society expects of us. Maybe the more we're around people who think we should want a career and money and all of that, the more we feel guilty if that's not really what makes us happy."

"Mom always said happiness was a choice. I believe that, but I also think that sometimes your circumstances really play a part in it as well."

"Maybe we can have joy without having our circumstances be perfect, but happiness has a little bit more to do with what's going on in our lives. It's hard to be happy when you're in the city alone, with no friends and a job you don't enjoy."

"Yeah. Although Mom said we could learn to enjoy our work no matter what we did. It was all part of our mindset."

"The more I hear about your mom, the wiser I think she is." Jubilee meant that with her whole heart. Because she had to admit she agreed with Lana that a person was pretty much about as happy as what they chose to be, regardless of their circumstances.

"So what I try to do is follow the chart that you see on this website. I'll send it to you. What's your phone number?" Clara said as she pulled out her phone and pulled up a website.

Jubilee gave it to her, and soon her phone pinged with the website information for weather and frost dates along Lake Michigan.

"You notice that there is a variation. Some years we're early, some years we're late. But I just try to use that as a guide. So for now, these are all the things I have planted. Have you ever raised plants in a garden before?" Then she laughed. "You must have, if you know that you enjoy weeding."

"I have. And I recognize the onions and the carrots and the beets." Jubilee continued to rattle off the things that she saw, pointing to them so that Clara would know she wasn't making it up.

They decided Clara would work on planting the beans and pumpkin seeds she had, while Jubilee worked on weeding.

"It's past time to go to the greenhouse and get pepper and tomato plants to plant. I rotate every year, and last year, those two tubs had the early vegetables in them, so I figured I would put the peppers and tomatoes in them this year."

"All right. If you tell me where the greenhouse is, I can make a trip. If not today, maybe tomorrow. I'll have to talk to Lana and see if she had anything else planned for me."

"She usually puts a premium on the garden, unless there are rooms that need to be cleaned so she can flip them the same day."

"We're probably getting to that time of year."

"We are." Clara gave her the directions on how to get to the greenhouse and told her the type of tomatoes and peppers she usually got. She texted them to her so that Jubilee wouldn't forget, and then she knelt down, and they worked in silence for a while.

"Am I being too nosy if I ask why you landed in Strawberry Sands? I mean, it's not exactly the type of place people flock to. And I could be wrong, but you didn't grow up here."

"No. I didn't. I spent one summer here. My aunt raised me after my mom left. I was just a baby."

"Your dad?"

"I saw him a couple of times growing up. Haven't talked to him for years. I wouldn't recognize him if I saw him on the street."

"Does your aunt live here now?" Clara asked, wrinkling her nose like she was trying to think of who of all the ladies in town might be her aunt.

"No. She passed away a few years ago. It was hard because that was really all the home I ever knew."

"That's sad." Clara gave a humorous laugh. "That makes my decision as to whether or not I should go to the Cities a little clearer. After all, I still have a home, a mom who loves me and who wants me to stay here. A place where I feel anchored. Plus, a whole pile of siblings that I know I can depend on for anything. Do you have siblings?"

"No. It was just me." Her dad might have had more children. But she'd never met any of them, and while she probably wouldn't mind meeting them, she couldn't imagine that she would feel any kind of connection to them since she didn't feel any kind of connection to her dad.

"I'm a little jealous of that. I wish I had your kind of grounding, you know?"

"Yeah. It's so much a part of what I think about myself. The idea that I have a family who loves me and supports me no matter what."

Jubilee didn't really want to talk about that anymore. She didn't really pity herself. And her life was just her life. It wasn't until she got older that she thought about what it might be like if she had a real family. People that she could depend on. She had wanted that for her girls. But...that hadn't worked out. That might have been part of the reason she moved in with her mother-in-law. Just hoping that everything would work out. That her husband would apologize, that they would make up, get back together, and be a family for her girls.

She didn't even care about being in love or whatever with her husband. She just wanted to have a family.

Sometimes it seemed like the harder a person worked for something, the more elusive it became. Maybe that was because she was trying to have a family in place of God, rather than allowing Him to be her anchor in the world.

Maybe He kept moving what she wanted, making it impossible to attain, so that she eventually turned to Him.

It was an idea that she tucked away to think about later. After all, it could be true. God wanted her to look to Him for her anchor, for her base, for her security. Not to family and friends.

Although He did provide family and friends for that purpose for a lot of people. He just hadn't done it for her.

She didn't want to resent that. She wanted to think that He did it to be an extra blessing to her. To make her have an even deeper and more vibrant relationship with Him, since she didn't have the typical family relationships that most people did.

"So, you can tell me if I'm being too nosy, but Matt doesn't typically do anything with anyone. With girls anyway. And you said you're going riding with him tonight. That makes me curious. Do you and Matt know each other somehow?"

Clara's voice seemed studiously uninterested, casual, but it made Jubilee want to smile because she was obviously very curious.

"I'm not sure. I knew him the summer I was here. Actually, I didn't know him know him. I don't even know if we ever talked. I think I would remember it if we had. I just admired him, because I remember him being handsome and nice. I remember seeing him ride along the shore of Lake Michigan and just thinking how neat it would be to be with him. You know, teenage crush. It's almost like a celebrity crush where there was never any chance of us being together. I was younger, first of all, and not the kind of girl who would catch Matt's eye."

"I don't know about that. Matt usually was pretty solid. He didn't get carried away by a pretty face or girls in bikinis. He was always rather strong and silent. You know that kind. Which makes it so odd that he..." Clara looked around a bit as though just remembering that Eva had been renting a room from her mom. "Eva really chased him. Shamelessly almost. I don't think Matt really liked her, and that made Mom complacent, I think. That and the fact that he was always so dependably good."

That was interesting to hear.

"Mom thinks she's back because she wants to get Matt back. Or get Matt to begin with, since she never really had him. Not that I really know what happened that summer. I just know Matt never acted like someone who was head over heels for someone. The next thing we knew, he had a child."

"I can't believe that he didn't offer to marry her." That seemed like something that he'd do, if he was as dependable as he seemed.

"I think he was going to. I don't think he really wanted to, but that's what he felt he should do? If that makes sense. But he did something that made Eva mad. She wouldn't talk to him, and Matt didn't really try to work things out. Again,

I think it was mostly because he didn't really care. She picked up with some other dude, and I'm not even sure he knew that she was pregnant. It was that fast. She wasn't showing. Next thing we knew, she was married and moving to Chicago. There were a few other men in there, but Matt insisted on visitation rights, and that's how they worked things out that he got Nora during the summer and a couple of weeks here and there during the school year."

Clara shrugged her shoulders. "He probably wouldn't appreciate me saying all of that, but it's common knowledge in our family. Now that Eva is back, people are probably going to be talking about it."

"Maybe he'll fall for her this time."

"I don't think so. She's not his type."

"She must've been a little bit his type."
They had a child together anyway.

"I think Eva just tried to be whatever
she thought Matt wanted. But regardless, she's very much the type that you
and I were just talking about a bit ago.
The corporate type. The kind of person
who tries to climb the ladder and tries to
fight and struggle for everything."

"Maybe she'd be looking for someone a
little more successful than Matt?" Jubilee
suggested as she carefully pulled a particularly stubborn weed out while trying
not to disturb the onions that were settled around it.

"Probably. Although, I don't know that
Matt isn't successful in the eyes of the

world. It's not like he's rich. He just has a good life, you know?"

Yeah. The kind of life that was the envy of so many people, that only came through hard work. It's just most people didn't see the hard work. They just saw the end result, horse rides on the beach, a cottage by the lake, a great family.

"You know, I guess maybe after talking to you, I've decided that I don't really want to move to the Cities. Although, I don't know if I even want to stay in my current job, even though it's nice to be able to work from home."

"What do you want to do?" Jubilee asked, curious.

"I always wanted to be an artist. You know, a starving artist. So that's why I haven't done that. I... I want to be able to eat too, you know?" Clara laughed. But Jubilee didn't.

"I keep hearing about how Blueberry Beach is getting bigger and the spillover is coming here. People are showing up in Strawberry Sands, and I hear it's getting busier every year. Maybe before things get super expensive, you could see about renting one of the empty storefronts on Main Street and set up a shop. You know, one of those quirky, touristy, cute shops tourists love. With overpriced artwork and an artsy vibe."

"Overpriced? Are you saying my work isn't worth anything?" Clara laughed, clearly teasing.

"You know what I mean." They laughed.

"I sure do. The kind of place where normal people probably wouldn't normally go, but they do on vacation, and they buy things not knowing what they're worth. Or they just buy something because they want something to remind them of their vacation to hang in their living room."

"Exactly. Something unique. Something that the rest of the world doesn't have. You know, that wasn't picked up at some big box store, and seventeen thousand people all have hanging over their mantle."

"Yeah. That kind of art."

"You should do it."

"You almost make me feel like I could."

"You won't know until you try."

Clara was quiet for a little bit, and as Jubilee looked over, she saw that she made her raised bed look like a work of art. Rows were perfectly aligned, the holes exactly spaced apart. Everything looking like it had been done with an artist's eye.

"I think it'd be really good. And weren't we just talking about you having all the siblings and family and friends that would rally around you if you fail?"

"I do. But I don't fail on purpose. After all, I want my siblings to be proud of me, not picking me up off the ground crying because my latest venture didn't work out."

"Don't they all know that you love being an artist? Don't they all know this would be a dream of yours? Don't you think they'd want you to reach for it?"

Clara sighed. "I'd like to think that. But don't you think that there's still people who would like to see me fail? Maybe not my siblings, but people who just get that kind of enjoyment when someone that they know tries something, maybe even something that they're afraid to do, and they just kind of hope in their heart that it doesn't work out because they want to be able to point and laugh a little. Maybe someone else's calamity makes them feel better."

"Are you going to allow people like that to hold you back?" Jubilee asked, wondering if that was part of her problem. After all, she stuck in her marriage for a long time, and maybe it was partly because she didn't want to admit that it didn't work out. She'd left her marriage and then lived with her mother-in-law, like she didn't want to admit that it didn't work out.

That was really for her girls, though.

"You know, you should do this before you have a husband and children who are depending on you. It would be a lot harder to do it then, wouldn't it?"

"I'll never get married."

"Why?" Jubilee asked. Although now that she'd been married, now that it hadn't worked out, she certainly wasn't sure she wanted to do it again. After all, when she was doing something where the success depended not just on her, but on someone else, she understood now that she couldn't make it work just because she wanted it to. She needed the person that she married to want to make it work too.

How did she know she was finding someone like that? She didn't want to screw up her daughter's lives any more.

Then why did she agree to go for a ride with Matt on the beach? If she wasn't interested in anything, shouldn't she be avoiding things like that?

She thought about that question the rest of the afternoon while Clara and she worked and considered it some more as

she helped Lana with supper preparations.

Matt and Nora showed up for supper, and Eva came up the stairs as well. That gave Jubilee a chance to see what Clara said about Eva was accurate. Eva defi-nitely had her eye on Matt.

She determined that at some point she would tell Matt she'd changed her mind about going riding and that she shouldn't have said yes in the first place. Not if she wasn't planning on being more than friends with anyone. It would lead him on or at the very least give everyone the wrong idea.

<h1 style="text-align:center">Chapter 12</h1>

Matt had to admit he'd been looking forward to supper and the beach horseback ride with Jubilee all day while he mowed hay in the afternoon and planned on tedding it in the morning and baling it the next day if it was dry enough.

But he wasn't as focused on the hay as he normally would have been. He was more focused on Jubilee and thinking about their ride. He'd actually gone down to his neighbors, Davis and Kim, and asked to borrow one of their horses. He wasn't sure where Jubilee's abilities were and how long it had been since she'd ridden, and he didn't want anything to happen to her. Their horses were slightly calmer and more dependable, and he wanted everything to be perfect for Jubilee.

His heart sank when he saw Eva was going to be eating supper with his mom. He figured that was probably the way things were going to go for the summer, since she was there.

He wished his mom would have told her no, that she needed to find a differ-ent place to live, but if she had done that, she wouldn't really have been his mom. Since his mom never turned anyone away. He would have thought over the years that she would have run out of money, constantly giving to people, but it seemed like the more she gave, the more God blessed her. And she always had enough. Always had enough for herself, always had enough to share with someone else.

He didn't ask if Eva was paying for her room, but he hoped his mom at least got something out of her.

He managed to avoid her for all of thirty seconds before she walked to him while his mom and Jubilee continued the supper preparations.

"Matt. I heard you guys were going on a horse ride this evening. I was hoping

I could tag along. I thought Nora was probably going as well, and it would be such a fun family thing to do," Eva said as she settled down to the right of him at the table. He was still standing behind his chair, looking to see if there was anything that he could help put on the table.

Eva had eaten a few times with them over the years and knew that the end of the table was his spot anytime he ate with his mom.

Clara and Jubilee seemed like they had become best friends, and they were both giving things to Scarlett and Penelope and Nora as well so that all the girls could help fill up the table with food.

He was tempted to go somewhere else and sit, just because he didn't want to spend the meal with Eva, but it would have been too conspicuous for him to leave the seat. How could he make it so that Jubilee would sit on the other side?

But if she did that, it might be uncomfortable for everyone. He wouldn't wish an awkward meal like that on anyone. He'd seen Eva's jealous and bad side.

He didn't really want it directed at Jubilee.

"Matt? Did you hear me?" Eva said, and her voice was laced with irritation, despite the smile on her face. She blinked her eyes at him as he looked down at her.

What had she said?

"I wanted to go on a horse ride with you tonight, along with Nora. It will be a nice family thing to do."

"I would love that!" Nora said, setting lettuce for their hamburgers down on the table in front of him. "Daddy, please?" She looked so eagerly at him, and then at her mother, then back at him. Like he had the power to restore their family. Like there was ever a family to begin with. It made him feel guilty. Guilty that Nora didn't have a family, guilty that she wanted one.

"Sure," he said, knowing that he probably should have checked with Jubilee. "If it's okay with Jubilee. I asked her first."

"Actually, I was thinking about not going. It's been a big day, with going to the lake and swimming, working in the garden and all the baking and all the things we did. You guys go on ahead. I think I'll probably call it an early night." She smiled and didn't seem upset. In fact, if he had to guess, maybe she seemed relieved.

Was she relieved that she didn't have to go with him? Was she dreading having to spend time with him? He kinda thought she looked eager to do it when he'd asked.

She had talked about it like it was something she wanted to do. He honestly had to admit he'd been looking forward to it all day. More than he normally looked forward to anything. Mostly because everything that he'd done with Jubilee had been fun, not fun in a super exciting teenager kind of way. But it was fun in a he'd enjoyed the companionship kind of way. The way he felt like he was with someone who wasn't going to stab him in the back the first time he did something wrong, someone who'd give him grace and would see past his faults and who was trustworthy enough for him to allow her to see past the exterior that he showed everyone else. That was how he felt about Jubilee.

Was it terrible that he wasn't really excited about riding with his daughter and her mother? That he didn't really want them to be a family. That he didn't see them as a family.

"It's hard to keep up with everyone around here. Maybe you'll develop some stamina after you've been here for a while," Eva said in a slightly condescending tone, although he imagined that it wasn't quite as condescending as it might have been, since she got what she wanted, with Jubilee backing out.

Eva held a conversation with him all through supper. Or maybe it was more like Eva chatted all through supper, and all he had to do was eat and nod his head.

Nora sat on the other side of him, and she seemed excited and happy that her mom and dad were talking and sitting at the same table with her.

As for Matt, he kept trying to see what was going on with Jubilee, who was carrying on a conversation with his mom and sister at the other end of the table. Her girls were involved in that conversation, their own conversation, and chatting with Nora as well.

At least it looked like Nora was going to have friends this summer.

Supper didn't end soon enough, and after Matt helped carry the dishes to the sink, where his mom was putting them in the dishwasher, while Jubilee and the girls put the food away, he walked out onto the porch.

Eva followed him out.

He wished he wouldn't have left the safety of the kitchen.

Thankfully Clara came out before Eva had a chance to say more than, "It's a beautiful evening. I can't wait for our ride. Do you want me to grab Nora so we can go down and get saddled up?"

He opened his mouth to reply, when Clara said, "Why don't you go do that. I wanted to talk to Matt for a minute anyway."

Eva went back in the house, calling Nora's name. Matt would have said to let her finish helping. It was good for her to do that, but Clara grabbed him by the arm and said, "Take a walk with me."

He allowed her to pull him, even though she was his little sister and he didn't typically follow her around.

He wasn't quite sure how his evening had gotten so messed up, from looking forward all day to being with Jubilee, to ending up going with Eva and dreading the fact that Nora was going to get ideas in her head about them getting together, when he had no such plans.

"You know that Eva is just trying to get her claws into you."

"I don't know why," he mumbled as they walked up the sidewalk, away from the lake.

"I'm not sure why either. It's not like you're super rich or anything like that. And it's not like she wants the best for Nora. Although it's obvious that Nora wants the two of you together as well."

"Yeah. I feel bad about that. Nora and I are going to have to have a talk. Because if that's what she wants, it's not going to happen."

"You let Eva push between you and Jubilee."

"You heard her. She didn't want to go anyway."

"She didn't want to go with you and your ex. The woman you have a child with. To be the third wheel in your family time."

He didn't point out that she would have been the fourth wheel, with Nora along. It seemed silly to split hairs like that. After all, Clara was trying to help. "What was I supposed to say? Nora was looking at me like it was the thing that she wanted more than life itself, and it felt rude to tell her no."

"If you ask Jubilee to go, then it should be you and Jubilee making the decision as to whether or not anyone else should go. It should have been you and her doing it together, in private. It shouldn't have been you asking her at the table in front of everyone. What else was she going to say?"

He knew that. He knew he'd messed up. He just...didn't have enough of a chance to think before he had to make a decision to say something.

"So what do I do now?"

It was too late to go back and fix anything. He had to move forward and try to fix it, but he didn't have any idea what to do.

"I'm not sure." Clara stopped and turned on the sidewalk to face him. "I don't know Jubilee that well. I mean, I just spent the day with her, but I only met her this morning. But she seems like a really nice person. Like the kind of person that I'd love to have as a sister-in-law."

"Whoa. I was thinking about a ride on the beach. I wasn't thinking about anything else."

"So now you just take rides on the beach with random women for the kicks and giggles? Is that really all you are?" She put her hands on her hips, and he had to look away from the gaze that she gave him.

He had never been the kind of person who just did things for the fun of it. That was part of the reason he hadn't dated much. He didn't want to just go out and have a good time, with no thought of the future. He always had marriage in the back of his head. That wasn't typical in today's day and age. He didn't fit into the casual dating scene, with most people looking for hookups and not for lifelong relationships.

"No. But I guess... I guess I wasn't think-ing anything more than a fun evening with someone that I liked. Maybe just to get to know her better."

"All right. That sounds a little better. I don't know what to do. I just wanted to make sure that you understood that Eva hasn't changed."

"I agree." It wasn't that he didn't think that people could change. He thought they could. But the fact that she was separated from the man that she had been with for the last five or six years made him feel like she was simply looking for someone else to latch onto.

"Maybe she's the kind of person who is insecure by herself, who needs to have a man. I don't know. I would just be careful with her."

"I didn't really need the warming, but I suppose it just says that you care. Thanks."

"Of course I care." Clara smiled. "You're my brother."

"I know." He tilted his head. "You seem pretty smitten with Jubilee."

"There's something...kind about her. She seems like an old soul. Gentle and... It makes me want to protect her."

"She reminds me of Mom."

"Yeah. She reminds me of Mom too. Not exactly, but those tendencies are there." Clara smiled, like that was all she needed to hear him say. And she knew he would do the right thing after that.

He wasn't entirely sure that her confidence wasn't misplaced, but he was going to try.

"I guess I'll go tell Eva and Nora that I'm not going for a ride," he said as they turned and started back toward the house.

"That's up to you. I... I would just make it clear that you're not getting together."

He nodded, knowing that he was going to have to explain to Davis why he didn't use his horse and a whole bunch of other things if he didn't take a ride. But he didn't like the way Eva had manipulated things, whether she meant to or whether she didn't, and he didn't want her to think that she could do it again. If he let her get away with it this time, not only would Nora have a false sense of hope, but Eva would be empowered to try again.

"Have a good evening," Clara said as she left him on the sidewalk to walk around the back of the house. Probably to look at the garden. That was her favorite spot anyway.

Lana and Jubilee were sitting on the porch with tall glasses of iced tea while Jubilee's girls played in the side yard on the swing.

Eva and Nora stood on the porch, watching him walk toward them.

As soon as Clara cut away, Nora started down the steps eagerly, with Eva coming slightly slower.

Jubilee glanced up, met his eyes for a second, and then looked away.

He wanted to talk to her more than anything, but he figured that he would take this opportunity to talk to Eva and Nora.

"Are you ready, Dad? Can I ride Boots?" Nora said, coming up to him and grabbing his hand.

He hadn't seen her except a couple of times at a few school events since she'd been at his house for a week over Easter. He didn't want to lose this evening with her, although he knew there would be plenty more evenings over the summer.

"Well, I think maybe I need to talk to you and your mom."

Eva tucked her hand into the crook of his arm on his other side and tugged gently, urging him forward past the front porch, back down the walk, and onto the sidewalk.

He wished he could feel Jubilee's eyes following them, but he had the impression that it didn't matter if they spontaneously combusted on the walk, she wouldn't look.

He didn't blame her. Clara was right. He had asked her to go with him, and he should not have allowed Eva to push her way in. At the very least, he should have checked with her privately before he changed their plans.

Trying to figure out whether he should talk to Eva with Nora or without her, he finally decided he'd start with his daughter.

"Nora, I feel like maybe I haven't been clear, and I wanted to make sure that you understand that I want to be friends with your mom. I want to get along with her. But we're never going to get together." He didn't want to be harsh, and he hated hurting his daughter more than anything, especially since he didn't get to spend that much time with her to begin with. But he couldn't allow this to continue, and he couldn't allow her to hope for something that was most definitely not going to happen. Not ever.

"Matt. That's harsh. I think you could have done that a little bit more carefully." Eva sounded affronted, and her hand tightened on his arm, although she did not let go. He wished she would. He didn't want her to be connected to him.

"I don't want to be harsh. I want to be realistic. We can do things together. I think that we've tried hard to be friends over the years. But there is absolutely nothing else that is going to happen. And I think it's important for Nora to know that. I... I got the idea that she might be thinking that there were possibilities that aren't there. Is that right?" He allowed his voice to show his concern and made it as gentle as possible as he looked at his daughter. He wished he hadn't made the mistakes he had. He wished he could fix them now.

He knew without a shadow of a doubt that trying to get together with Eva was just going to end up in more heartache. For all of them. It was better to be honest and upright. Upfront.

"Why not, Daddy? You guys get along just fine. Why not live together? Why not be married and be a real mom and dad?"

Nora, his sweet little girl, had her chin jutted out in an irritated, stubborn way.

"Because your mom and I were never really together to begin with. We just screwed up and did things we shouldn't have. Sometimes when you do things you shouldn't have, it affects people that you don't even know it's going to. Like you. You are not a mistake. But your mother and I weren't married, we had no intentions of getting married. We didn't even like each other that much."

"Speak for yourself. I was in love. I knew you wouldn't have anything to do with me."

"That's news to me. You didn't say anything like that at the time. In fact, I think when we woke up the next morning, you were mad at me because I...slept on the wrong side of the bed. I'm pretty sure that's what the problem was."

"I don't remember anything about that."

He remembered her yelling at him because he'd left her on the side of where the door was, and she was afraid someone was going to see her if they walked in. She said if he had been a gentleman, he would have slept on the other side. She hopped out and hadn't talked to him for days. Which, honestly, hadn't bothered him much. Other than he wasn't sure what to tell his mom. Knowing that she would be disappointed in him. In fact, he decided not to tell her anything; he was twenty and was perfectly capable of doing things without his mother knowing about them.

He'd been acting as the man of the family for years, since his dad had left, and figured that he could make a mistake or two without having to admit it to everyone.

Turned out that wasn't true, since four weeks later, everyone knew about his mistake. Much to his chagrin. But there wasn't anything he could do about it then.

Nora turned stormy eyes on him. "Mom's willing to work things out. You are not. I don't know why you have to be such a jerk all the time." Nora crossed her arms over her chest. "Mom, you were right. He's a big jerk." She looked down her nose at him and pulled up her lip. "I don't know why I idolized him so much when I was younger. If this is the way you're going to be, I want to live with Mom."

"Hold on. You're not old enough to make that decision. Your mom and I have decided where you're going to be, and you need to abide by our decisions until you're older."

He held onto his temper with both hands. He didn't want to dump all over Eva, but it was obvious that she was filling Nora's head with a bunch of lies and trying to get Nora to gang up on him with her.

"I'm sorry. I'm sorry that things didn't work out. But that's the way life goes for people. I didn't want my dad to leave, but he did. Maybe there were things my mom could have done to keep him. But him leaving gave me the opportunity to grow up faster, shoulder responsibility, and become a man of integrity and character, the opposite of what he was. I don't blame him for leaving, and I don't hate him. I just admire what my mom did after he left, raising all six of her children alone."

"I hear you. So you had a really hard life. So did I. But you are standing here in front of me, and you could make my life better, and you refuse to."

Eva looked smug as Nora stood there with her hands crossed over her chest.

He focused on Eva. "I think it might be a good idea for you to find a different place to stay. If this is the way you're going to try to drive a wedge between my daughter and me. This time, summer, is supposed to be my time with her. I'm willing to share it, I'm willing to have you be here, but not if this is the way things are going to go."

His voice sounded reasonable, even though he was boiling inside. He wanted to take a hold of Eva, grab her by her throat and shake her. How could she have done this? He had a really great relationship with his daughter all through her school years, her childhood. He'd made sure of it. And now, now that Eva had left her husband and set her sights on him, apparently, and she wasn't getting what she wanted, she was going to try to destroy everything he had.

He supposed that she could probably be successful. Nora didn't look inclined to be the little girl that he'd known all of her life. She looked inclined to be the spitting image of her mother.

It made him sad.

It made him regret the mistakes he made and wish he could redo them, but of course that was impossible.

"Nora, I think you and I need to walk home. Eva, I'll talk to my mom if I need to, but you need to find someplace else to stay. Have a great night." He looked at Nora and lifted his brows, just to see if she was going to argue.

She set her face, glanced at her mom, but didn't wait for permission before she turned her back and started marching down toward the beach and his cottage.

"Eva. I've never said a single bad word to her about you. And you know as well as I do that there's plenty I could say. Times you were late, times you cheated me, times I gave you money. Times where I had to take care of Nora because you were running around with a man who wasn't your husband. Nora never knew anything about those things."

He shut his mouth. He could tell from the look on Eva's face that it was a waste of time to try to talk to her. She felt she was in the right, and it didn't matter what he said.

He shook his head. He wanted to tell her to make sure that she found another place to stay, but he'd already said it twice.

Disgusted that the evening hadn't turned out the way he had hoped and heartsick that his daughter was upset with him, he turned and walked down the street. Hopefully, he could talk to Nora and they could come to some kind of agreement. Or at least, he could convince her that he wasn't trying to ruin her life.

Maybe her mother had already poisoned her brain, and there wasn't going to be anything he could do other than just act with integrity and character, and hope that eventually, as she got older, she'd see that Eva was the one who wasn't telling the truth.

He said a short prayer, one that pleaded with the Lord to keep his relationship with his daughter intact. He didn't want to lose her. He wanted her to know how much she meant to him, and he wanted to have influence in her life. Wanted to help her not make the mistakes he had, and wanted her to feel loved and cherished.

Chapter 13

Clara had warned Jubilee that she would be roped into doing something the moment she stepped in the church.

Clara had been wrong.

It hadn't been the moment she stepped in, she had ten minutes of being introduced to new people, and chatting with Davis and Kim and oohing and aahing over Kathleen, before she got roped into something.

"Welcome to Strawberry Sands. I hear you're helping Lana at the bed-and-breakfast," a voice said from behind her as a hand landed on her shoulder. She straightened and turned around.

"Thank you. That's accurate."

"I'm Bethann, and I'm head of the Strawberry Festival committee. I'm hoping I can recruit a new member."

"Me?" Jubilee said, even though she was pretty sure that was what Bethann was saying.

"Well yeah. If you're going to be here all summer long, we can't have you sitting around when there's work to be done, now can we?" she said, and she made it sound like common sense.

"I would love to help," Jubilee said, although her voice lacked conviction.

"That's exactly what I thought when I saw you. I'm going to put you down on the entertainment committee. It will be your committee's job to find people to perform for those three days, Friday evening, Saturday all day, and Sunday after church. We try to get religious groups on Sunday, just keep that in mind." Bethann rattled things off as though Jubilee was standing there with a notepad in her hand, taking notes. Her brain felt a little fried. "I've already gotten you a cochair, and in addition to finding groups to provide entertainment for those three days, you will also rent the equipment, including the sound system, the stage, and chairs for visitors. You'll coordinate the parking and take care of anything else, including vendors, particularly food vendors, since people will be hungry and thirsty, and anything else that needs to be done for those things." Bethann looks satisfied with herself, like it was a hard job to dump a bunch of stuff from her shoulders onto Jubilee's. Which was exactly what happened.

"Oh. And there's your cochair." Bethann waved a hand and said, "Eva! I have your cochair. You two need to get together. Don't forget, I'll send you a link to the budgets for everything, and you'll know exactly how much money you have to work with. You have to get checks from our treasurer, who I still have to track down and inform her of her job. So, expect a text from me about that. All right. You two can have an impromptu meeting I'm sure before church. You've got," she looked at her watch, "seven minutes."

She hurried off.

Jubilee had wanted to interrupt her ever since she'd waved Eva down and informed her that that was her cochair.

Supper last night had been awkward. To say the least. Especially after Eva had issued her veiled insult about Jubilee not being able to keep up with the work around the place.

Kind of funny since Eva had napped all afternoon while Jubilee had taken her children to the beach and then worked in the garden before coming in to help with supper.

She hadn't said anything. That would have only started an argument, and one she probably could have won, but one that she didn't want to have. Supper wasn't meant for arguments; supper was meant for families to get together and laugh and enjoy each other's company.

"I'll tell her that I can't do it," Eva said, her lip pulled back, her eyes on the ground.

Jubilee wasn't sure whether it was her posture or the dejection in her words, or maybe it was just because Jubilee always had a tendency to see the good in everyone.

Eva wanted Matt, and she was only doing what she did to try to get him.

It wasn't Eva's fault that Matt had gone along with it, although Jubilee had heard from Clara that she didn't think Matt was actually going to go riding with Eva and Nora. She'd gone to bed and didn't know if they had or not. And she told herself she didn't care.

Jubilee hadn't been sure how she felt about that anyway. After all, Nora was such a sweet girl, and of course she wanted her parents to be together. Jubilee wanted that for them. If it had been her own girls longing for her to be back with her husband, even though her husband had cheated and treated her terribly, it would be tempting for her to do that. Just to make her girls happy.

Thankfully, her husband had been just as unkind to her girls as he had been to her. Neither one of them had ever breathed a word about wanting her to go back to him.

She dreaded the idea that they might, although she knew that time seemed to heal all wounds, and it made things that were bad at the time seem not so bad with the rosy glow of hindsight.

Regardless, she didn't want to borrow trouble, but she understood where Matt was coming from.

Even though there was a part of her, a part of her that wanted to be admired and appreciated as a woman, a part of her that was a little bit petty and needy, who was offended that Matt had told her that he would go riding with her and then allowed Eva to invite herself onto their excursion, most of her understood that she and Matt weren't really going on a date. They were just doing something fun together. And why not bring his daughter and his ex?

It wasn't like he was trying to put them into their relationship. They didn't have a relationship, so he could hardly do that.

"Eva."

Eva looked up at her.

"If you don't want to work with me, that's fine. But if it's something that you'd like to do, I'm okay with it. We can do this together. I think it would actually be kind of fun, although..." Her brows crinkled. "I feel like Bethann railroaded me into it. Is that what she did to you?"

Eva laughed. "If you consider railroading having someone come up to me and say, 'you look like the perfect person to cochair this committee, and I'm going to find you a cochair to do it along with you, and you're just going to love it, so get used to the fact that you're going to be doing it,'" Eva imitated Bethann almost exactly, "then yeah. I think I was railroaded."

Jubilee laughed. "All right. That makes two of us. Still, I was kind of looking for a reason to get involved in the town and looking for a way to get to know people. This feels like a good one, if you're up for it?" She gave an encouraging smile, not one that was condescending but one she hoped was friendly and kind, that wasn't slobbering, that wasn't begging, but also wasn't lording it over her either.

It must have done the trick, because Eva grinned. "Sounds good."

"All right. So, we are down to four minutes." Jubilee glanced at her watch. The pianist had just started to play the prelude. "Do you want to meet at the diner after the service? I heard a rumor already this morning that Griff whipped up another batch of strawberry cheesecake, and they would be serving until it was gone this afternoon. What do you think?"

"What about your girls?" Eva asked, a little bit of a shadow crossing her eyes.

Maybe because she wouldn't have been kind if Jubilee hadn't taken the first steps.

"Lana, she's so sweet, asked if she could have them this afternoon. I haven't had a chance to take them on a horse ride, and she was going to go to Davis and Kim's stable and rent some of their beginner horses for the girls. They're so excited."

"And you are going to go?"

She actually had been going to go. She'd wanted to ride since she'd gotten to Strawberry Sands, but after the debacle of the previous evening when Matt had asked her and Eva had pushed in, she'd given up on that pursuit. Particularly since it meant having to deal with

Matt, whom she managed to avoid since then.

"Nope. I have the afternoon free. And strawberry cheesecake sounds like a really nice way to spend an afternoon. If that's okay with you?"

"It is... Jubilee?"

"Yeah?" Jubilee said, having already taken one step away, toward the pew where Scarlett and Penelope sat with Nora and Lana.

"Thank you. You could have been...unkind. Or, at the very least, refused to work with me. I appreciate it."

"No problem," Jubilee said. She didn't think Matt would agree, but she couldn't blame Eva for wanting Matt back. For wanting Matt to begin with. He was obviously a good man. A hard worker, someone with a sense of humor, and someone who truly loved his daughter. All things that Jubilee would admire in a man. She also thought he would probably be faithful, although she thought that about her ex-husband too, and she'd been wrong.

She was tempted to turn back to Eva and tell her that she wasn't really interested in getting together with anyone, and Eva didn't have anything to worry about her wanting anything to do with Matt, but she decided that that would just be overkill. She kept her mouth shut. She wasn't entirely sure that she trusted Eva to be her very best friend, but she thought they could get along well enough to work together for the festival at least.

Especially since Bethann had no idea of what had been going on as far as Jubilee knew, and it was the Lord who allowed them to be put together. Maybe He just wanted to see if Jubilee was going to love the way God wanted her to love. A big love. A love that overlooked faults and insults and petty hurts. A love that took someone who was unkind, or even be-trayed her, and loved them anyway. The way Jesus loved his disciples, the way God loved the world before He sent His son for it.

That was the kind of love that gar-nered attention, that was the kind of love that made people look at a person and know that they were a Christian, because someone could love that way.

Maybe she would be successful. She'd messed up her life so often, and she definitely wasn't feeling that kind of love toward her ex, although she worked through a lot of the bitterness and hurt and had been more than willing to forgive and forget. That took a certain amount of love.

Up until they signed the divorce papers, she would have taken him back.

Now that the divorce was final, she could love him from a distance. And focus instead on loving the people directly in her life, with the kind of love with which God loved her.

Chapter 14

Nora sat in church with her arms crossed over her chest. Her dad had forced her to go that morning. She hadn't wanted to, but he hadn't given her a choice. It was America. She was supposed to be free to do whatever she wanted to, not forced to have religion crammed down her throat she didn't want to. Her mom didn't make her go to church.

Dad was just being a jerk. He knew she wanted her mom and him to be a family, and he was just deliberately not doing it because he hated her.

She could see that now.

She didn't pay any attention to the service. While she normally liked church, she was mad because her dad made her go, so she didn't pay attention, and when it was over, she ran to her nana.

At least someone around there appreciated her. She didn't even have to say anything, but as she approached, Nana opened her arms wide, and Nora stepped into them, loving the cinnamon and vanilla scent that always clung to her and burying her head in her shoulder. For some reason, feeling her arms squeeze her tight made her want to cry.

Why did life have to be so hard? Why couldn't her parents just get along? Why couldn't they just be a family?

Her mom finally got away from the man she was living with. Nora didn't even call him her stepdad. He didn't like her. He had a kid of his own that visited on the weekends sometimes, and that's who he really liked. Nora was just in the way.

"You're coming home with me, aren't you?" Nana said, pulling back a little bit to look down into her eyes.

She nodded belligerently, even though she liked Nana.

"What's the matter, Nora? Is there something wrong?"

"No."

She saw her new friends, Scarlett and Penelope, but she just waved to them and didn't go over and talk to them. But they walked over to them.

"Is it okay with you if Scarlett and Penelope eat with us?" Nana asked.

Nora wanted to say no, just because every answer that came out of her mouth wanted to be a no right now, but she liked Scarlett and Penelope.

"Are we having hot dogs in the backyard?" she asked.

"We can if you want to. I have some in the refrigerator, and I figured that we'd do it at some point. That's kind of our thing, isn't it?" Nana smiled and winked at her.

It was their thing. Usually the old oak tree in the yard lost a couple of branches over the winter, and her dad would cut them up and stack them along the fence. Nana had a few stones that formed a circle, and they put camp chairs around it and called it a fire pit.

It was one of her favorite things to do in Strawberry Sands. Other than ride horses and play in the lake of course.

"Are you coming to eat?" Nana asked, and Nora turned her head to see her dad walking over. He didn't look angry, he just looked...sad.

It almost made Nora feel guilty. She'd always loved her time with her dad. Summers by the lake were the best. And her dad let her do pretty much anything. Sometimes they stayed up until three o'clock in the morning watching movies and eating popcorn and drinking soda.

Her mom never let her stay up. Even though sometimes her mom and the man she married, George, stayed up late. They just never let Nora do it with them. It was like they wanted their own private time.

Which was fine with Nora. Except she never got her own private time with her mom.

"I'd like to, but I think I better go home. The horses need to be moved to the back pasture, and I need to fix the fence on the back corner piece."

That made Nora happy. At least she told herself that. Except, everything was more fun when her dad did it too. She didn't really want him not to do it. But she didn't want him there either. She wasn't sure what she wanted. She held Nana tighter and leaned her head against Nana's shoulder again.

"All right," Nana said. "It'll be Nora and Scarlett and Penelope and me." Nora could almost hear the twinkle in Nana's voice. "We might get some nice thunderstorms this afternoon, which will be fun."

It didn't matter what happened, Nana had a backup plan for her backup plan, and she always made sure they had fun. She almost asked if they could throw a blanket over the dining room table and have a fort inside if it rained, but Penelope and Scarlett might think that was too little girlish. She'd have to talk to them about it. Just broach it carefully, asking them to see what they thought, before she actually suggested it. She didn't want them to make fun of her for being a little girl. Even though she still liked to do little girl things sometimes. She was twelve, but she still packed a couple of dolls in her suitcase, just because she didn't want to spend the whole summer without them. Was it really fair that she had to leave all of her things at the storage unit that her mom rented? She didn't understand why George couldn't move out. Why did it have to be her and her mom? They always seemed to get the short end of the stick.

"After I move the horses, I can bring my ice-cream maker, and we can make some ice cream if you'd like."

Scarlett and Penelope both squealed. Nora managed to not squeal, and she thought she did a pretty good job of keeping the excitement that she felt off her face too. Her dad made the best ice cream in the world. It wasn't really even ice cream. It was more like custard. Like frozen cream that was just sweet enough to make her tongue dance and her mouth smile.

Sometimes he made raspberry ice cream, and that was the best.

She couldn't help herself. She said, "Do you have raspberries?"

He smiled, not a gloating kind of smile that he'd finally gotten her to talk, but a true happy smile like he was happy to talk to her. Sometimes her mom smiled a gloating smile, which made Nora determined that she wouldn't talk to her mom anymore or give in, but she always ended up doing it.

"I do. It's too early in the season for them, you know that. They're never ripe until July. But I have two bags that I saved from last summer when we went picking, just because I thought we might want raspberry ice cream this year before they were ready."

He smiled again like having raspberry ice cream with her made him happy.

She wanted him to be happy. But she wanted herself to be happy too. She would be happy if her parents were together.

Except what was that thing that Nana always said? That she couldn't depend on other people to make her happy. She had to decide to be happy for herself.

She could just hear Nana saying it now. Even years ago when she wished that her parents were together, Nana had said that. And she knew Nana knew what she was talking about because Nana's husband left her. She found out from other people that he was a cheater and a liar and he hadn't been nice to Nana at all.

And yet, Nana never complained about him. And she never blamed him for anything that happened. She just decided to be happy. If only it were that simple.

"Do you get to eat ice cream and cook hot dogs over a fire all the time?" Scarlett said as she hooked her arm with hers and they left the church together.

Penelope walked along on the other side, and she said, "A fire? You get to have a real fire?"

"Yeah. We have a fire in the little fire ring out in the yard. It's not a big fire."

"I don't think our mom would ever let us have a fire. In fact, we better not tell her." Scarlett looked across Nora at Penelope and raised her brows, as though warning her little sister not to say anything.

Just that made Nora sad. Why couldn't she have sisters? She didn't understand.

They had a good time that afternoon, with the fire and the hot dogs and even marshmallows, and Nana dug up candy bars for s'mores. And then, to top everything off, just as it started to rain, her dad brought his ice-cream machine, and they all went in the house and he made raspberry ice cream.

Her friends thought she was the luckiest person in the world, and she kind of felt that way too. Except after her friends left, and she begged her dad to let her stay with Nana, she felt sad and lonely again.

She wanted siblings. She wanted a family. She wanted a mom and dad who lived in the same house. Why couldn't she have that? Other people did.

"You've been kind of quiet all day. And this is one of your favorite things to do. The fire, the marshmallows, the hot dogs, and the raspberry ice cream. I think your dad makes it better every year."

"It was really good," Nora said, sitting in the sunroom, watching as the clouds cleared over the lake and the sun sank low. Pretty soon it would set, and if the clouds were just right, they'd glow orange and yellow and pink and flare up into the sky in a big beautiful sunset, the kind she loved watching in Strawberry Sands. Where her mom and she lived in Indiana, they didn't get sunsets like that. Or maybe they did, and she just couldn't see them because of all the other houses and buildings that were in the way.

"So what's going on? You look like someone stole your ice cream, but I know that's not true. I saw you eat it all yourself." Her nana touched her arm and then snuggled down in her chair, a blanket over her legs, her eyes on the sky, like she was looking forward to the sunset just like Nora.

"I want a family."

She could tell Nana anything. Nana understood.

"What about our family?"

"Like one that lives together. I want one like Penelope and Scarlett. They have each other. They're sisters. Why can't I have sisters? Why didn't God give me sisters?"

Nana sighed. She didn't say anything, but she just looked at the sky.

Maybe it was her quiet contemplation that made Nora go on.

"Why can't my mom and dad live together? I mean, they were together for a while. They had me. Why does Dad hate Mom?"

"Your dad doesn't hate your mom," Nana said right away. Even though Nana was her dad's mom, Nana never took sides. Not that Nora had ever really thought about her parents having sides. But as she thought back, Nana had always welcomed her mom just as enthusiastically as she welcomed her dad. Nana welcomed everyone. If she didn't know that her dad was Nana's son, she wouldn't have figured it out by the way Nana acted.

"I told you once a long time ago that my husband left me."

Nana's voice was soft, and it sounded a little bit far away. It made Nora sit up straighter, because Nana didn't usually talk about her husband and the problems that she had. It made her feel like she was almost an adult to have Nana confide in her like this.

She listened, saying, "You did."

"If he were to come back. Today." She looked over at Nora and smiled. "This very night. Say he would walk in the door right now." She raised her brows as though she were wondering if Nora was following her.

Nora nodded eagerly.

"I hope I would be nice to him. But I wouldn't want to go back with him. Do you understand?"

"Because he's a jerk."

"A little bit. I guess. But...the person I was when I was married is a different person than the one I am today. He asked me to marry him, and I was thrilled to say yes. I was excited to have a wedding. I felt my wedding day was the best day of my life in a beautiful dress and a handsome man who held my hand and made me feel beautiful."

She sighed a little and smiled, as though the memories of the day made her happy. "But because of everything that came after, or maybe because I'm not the girl I used to be. I wouldn't be honored if he came back and wanted to marry me. I've changed. I'm different. We tried it once, it didn't work, and I don't want to try again. I think I would welcome him into my home. I would treat him the way I would treat anyone else who would come. I hope. But if he asked me to try again with him, I would say no."

She gave Nora a look. A look that only Nana could give. One that was full of love and compassion and Nora could feel the desire of her nana to make her understand.

"I'm not saying he's a bad man. He might make someone else a really good husband. Maybe he's changed. Maybe he's the kind of husband that anyone would be happy to have. But...not me. He's not the husband for me."

She looked at Nora, thoughtfully, as though she were trying to think of something to say. "Do you remember when you used to come here and I used to feed you from the high chair? Remember how you used to sit in the booster seat? Do you remember how we had all the little safety gates and you had a little playpen that you played in sometimes?"

Nora nodded. She always loved coming to Nana's. She loved the summers where her dad carried her out in the night air, and she sat on his lap all snuggled up on the porch swing. Her sippy cup in one hand, her teddy bear in the other, and she'd fall asleep and somehow magically wake up in her bed in the cottage in the morning. It all felt beautiful and safe and happy.

"You don't want to go back to holding your sippy cup again? You don't want to play in the playpen. To sit in the booster seat. You've changed. You've grown up, of course, but you're not the little girl that you used to be. You couldn't go back even if you wanted to. You're too big for the booster seat. You don't fit. That happens in life sometimes. People were together, and then something happens, and they don't fit anymore. They couldn't go back even if they wanted to. I think that's probably the way it is with your dad and your mom. They didn't really work together much at all. In fact, I don't recall ever seeing them together that summer. But whatever they had, they didn't fit. They wouldn't work out. They'd probably end up fighting a lot, and you don't want to live in a house where all your parents do is fight with each other, right?"

Nora nodded, because her mom and George fought a lot, and even though George wasn't her dad, she hated it. She wanted to go hide every time there was yelling. It scared her for some reason. Even though she knew that neither one of them would hurt her. It wasn't her fault. She just hated it.

"But why can't they just be together and make themselves be happy, like you said?" Even though she understood what Nana said, it didn't change the fact that she wanted her parents to try.

"I don't think I ever said you could make yourself be happy," Nana said thoughtfully, like she was trying to remember exactly what she had said. "I think I said you could choose to be happy." She smiled a little. "Sometimes choosing to be happy also involves choosing to do or to not do certain things. For example, I'm afraid of heights, so if I want to be happy, I'm going to choose to not fly in an airplane, because I'm going to be scared. So it's kind of silly for me to do something that I know is going to make me struggle to try to be happy. I'm much happier with my two legs firmly on the ground." She pointed to her legs and her feet which sat flat on the floor.

"Or I might tuck them up like this," she said, kicking her flip-flops off and tucking her legs up in her chair the way Nana often did. "I'm not going to fly anywhere, unless it's absolutely necessary, because I'm not going to be happy while I'm doing it." She let out a breath. "That doesn't mean you never have to do anything you don't want to do. Sometimes we do. And sometimes we just have to knuckle down and decide to be happy anyway. But we don't deliberately put ourselves in a position we don't have to be in, especially if we know it's going to make us or the people around us miserable." She lifted her brows, and Nora knew she wanted her to understand.

That was the nice thing about Nana. Nana didn't care how long it took for Nora to get what she was trying to explain. Nana would explain forever and ever and never get tired. Her mom took about three minutes, and if Nora didn't get it, her mom got frustrated.

Her dad had a little bit more patience, but not much. Although, he taught her to ride horses, and she didn't recall him ever getting upset with her when she didn't get that the first time.

"Maybe you just are really looking for your mom and dad to get together because you're sad and upset that things didn't work out between your mom and George."

Nana often had a way of getting to the heart of the matter. She was upset about her mom and George. Even though she didn't really like George, he was still a dad in her house. She didn't feel quite so alone. Like her mom and she had someone else that they could depend on. It was scary for it to just be her and her mom.

"Maybe," she finally said, softly.

"I know it's hard. I wished a lot of times that my husband hadn't left, because my kids didn't have a dad. Your dad didn't have a dad. He knows what you're going through."

Nora wrinkled her nose and shook her head. She didn't want to hear about her dad knowing what she was going through, even though she knew Nana was right.

"He could talk to you about that. You know he could. He didn't, and all of your aunts and uncles, from Uncle Luke down to Aunt Clara. They all know what it's like to not have a dad."

"They had siblings at least."

"That's true. But there are times I think they wish they didn't have siblings, because when you have siblings, you have to share. There are good things and bad things with every situation. If you have a dad, there will be things that he's not going to let you do. Wasn't that true with George? Did he take up your mom's time and you didn't get to spend as much time with her because George was there?"

Nora nodded begrudgingly.

"I've been praying for years, not just for your mom, but for your dad too. Not really that they would get together, but that whatever happens with them, you will be safe and secure. I have a feeling that maybe the Lord is working things out. Not for your parents to get together, but for something else to happen for you." Nana smiled, like she knew something that Nora didn't, but Nora knew better than to ask. Nana wouldn't tell her. Not until she was sure it was going to happen.

"Do you think?" she asked instead.

"I do," she said, putting her arm around Nora and tucking her closer until Nora leaned her head against her chest, and they sat like that, while the sun lit up the sky.

Nana was always so sure that God was good. Even when Nora wasn't so sure. It made Nana happy to talk about it. But Nora kind of wondered that if God was so good, why did Nana's husband leave? Why didn't Nana have someone to love her? Why was her mom alone? Why didn't her dad have someone to love and take care of him?

Once she'd asked about it, and Nana had said something about sin in the world, and men making a choice to sin, and so then they had to live with the conse-quences.

Nora knew all about consequences, and she supposed being angry at her dad was pointless. After all, Nana wouldn't get back with her husband. She couldn't hardly expect her dad to do something Nana wouldn't do.

Even though she was disappointed, she understood. She wouldn't want to be forced to be with someone she didn't really like.

Although, she hoped that whenever she had children, she did the very best she could for them. That was important. She knew that much.

Chapter 15

Jubilee met with Eva at the diner, and they decided that Eva would be responsible for contacting people to perform, booking and scheduling them, while Jubilee would be responsible for everything else—the stage, the lighting, the speakers, the sound system, someone to run the sound system, parking, and vendors.

It seemed like a fair deal to Jubilee. She was excited about things that she planned to have and was grateful that she didn't have to worry about trying to contact and coordinate the schedules of performers.

Eva was going to take care of making sure they got paid as well. It felt like a win-win. They were working together, but they each had their own area, and it wouldn't step on each other's toes.

Eva had been decent to work with, and they had enjoyed their strawberry cheesecake. It had been the best strawberry cheesecake Jubilee had ever eaten, and she had made sure to tell Griff that. Every time she'd seen him, he was quiet, although not sullen or withdrawn. But today he seemed sad. She wasn't quite sure what that meant, but he smiled at her compliment, and it made her feel good that she'd brightened his day a little.

She couldn't help everyone with all the problems in the world, but it always felt like when she met someone who seemed to be carrying a burden, she wanted to try to ease it for them if she could. The compliment didn't solve any-thing, but they made a person smile, and that made her heart happy.

Her girls had had an amazing time with Lana, and they chattered about the ice cream that Matt had made, along with the fire and how they were allowed to roast their own marshmallows, and how Miss Lana didn't even care that they were close to the fire. The weather hadn't been conducive to horseback riding, with the possibility of thunderstorms looming on the horizon, but the girls hardly even noticed.

Jubilee thought that maybe she had been slightly overprotective, when her girls thought getting close to fire was something that might get them in trouble.

She thanked Lana before they had left, with the girls wanting to walk down to the lake for a little bit before bedtime.

Jubilee had suggested that, since she thought maybe Lana wanted some time alone with her granddaughter. She hoped that her girls weren't infringing on that time.

Matt had left earlier, after the ice cream had been eaten. The girls and Lana had been there, and Jubilee had been successful in keeping them between her and him.

She didn't want him cornering her and asking her why she had declined to go horseback riding with him, after she said she would. She didn't want to have to explain that she shouldn't have accepted in the first place. Part of her wanted to give him a hard time for allowing Eva to push her way into something that they'd planned. After all, he'd asked her, she said yes, and he hadn't said anything about taking anyone else.

His daughter, she could understand, but his ex? She was pretty sure she wasn't wrong in thinking that was something anyone would have been upset about.

Regardless, it helped her get her thinking straight and realize that she shouldn't have accepted to begin with, since she wasn't planning on anything happening between them. Therefore, it was rude of her to allow him to think any differently.

Still, that was a conversation she didn't want to have, and she was happy that she managed to avoid it for at least another day. The girls skipped and chattered ahead, while she walked along behind.

She smiled at how happy they were and how much fun they had, and she thanked the Lord for the welcome that they'd had here in Strawberry Sands.

She was going to have to work hard. Lana had shown her the schedule, and she knew that there were going to be guests every day the next week, some-times four or five a night. That meant a lot of cooking, a lot of cleaning, a lot of laundry, added to keeping the garden, and in between the cracks, she need-ed to schedule everything that she just agreed to handle for the Strawberry Fes-tival which wasn't that far away.

She'd already told the girls not to go into the water without her, and she had in her head that she wasn't going to let them get wet at all. It was cool now that the sun had gone down. They'd be shivering and cold by the time they got back to the bed-and-breakfast and sandy and dirty as well.

She was thinking about how she hoped that she wouldn't have to give them a bath before bed when she realized that the figure on horseback that she'd been idly watching was Matt.

She wished she could grab the girls and turn around and go power walking back to the bed-and-breakfast, just so he wouldn't see them. But there was no way she could do that as far beyond her as what the girls were. They'd never hear her over the crashing waves.

The sun hadn't quite made its descent into the horizon yet, and the world was still washed with the rain that they'd had that afternoon, and the man on horseback, no matter how she felt about the man himself, blended into the scene, making it absolutely perfect.

If she pretended it wasn't Matt, she could admire the beauty of the horse, the ease of the rider, and how he seemed to be at one with his animal, the flowing mane and tail, the proud tossing head, and the waves crashing in the background.

But no one had given the memo to her children that she didn't want to have Matt stop and talk to anyone, and as soon as they recognized him, they went running over.

She figured they were probably begging for him to take them for a ride at some point. Maybe she could circumvent Matt and go directly to Davis and Kim and take them up on their offer of allowing them to use their horses if they weren't rented out. She hated to not give them anything for their use, though, and the problem was, she wasn't getting paid until the next Friday, and at that point, she was going to have to figure out how to square up with Lana for all the things that Lana had been doing for her, and then she was going to have to try to keep back as much as she could so that she could not only rent the place over winter but have enough funds to see her through if she ended up losing her job.

If she kept thinking like that, worry would overtake her, so she tried to shove those thoughts aside. There would be plenty of time to worry while she worked in the coming week. Today was about enjoying the beach and the water and the waves and the sunset.

Except, all of the enjoyment was gone because Matt stopped, dismounting, nodding his head, and laughing with her girls.

Before she knew it, the girls had turned around and raced back up the beach while Matt stood holding the reins of his horse. He didn't walk toward her but just watched as her girls ran with a smile on his face.

"Mr. Matt said that he'd take us for a ride. Just lead us on his horse. That way, we don't have to worry about his horse running away with us. He said that we could both ride at the same time, but he said we couldn't do it unless you said it was okay." Penelope had beaten her older sister to her, and she had all of that out before Scarlett stopped running.

"Please, Mom, can we let Mr. Matt take us for a horse ride? I promise that we'll be good, and we aren't imposing, 'cause he asked. We didn't ask him. We just said we wanted to go. He said how about now? But then he wouldn't take us unless we came to you and asked."

Scarlett was usually the less pushy of the two girls, but both of them had begging looks on their faces, and Jubilee didn't think she had it in her heart to say no.

She wanted to give her girls every good thing, loved that Lana had taken them and given them such a great day. She hated to say no, just for spite, just because she didn't want to have to deal with Matt. Not because there was any reason that her girls couldn't do it.

So she nodded and said they could have a five-minute ride, then they were going back up to the bed-and-breakfast. If she was careful, she could avoid talking to Matt at all.

Chapter 16

Matt tried to watch for a time where he could have a chance to talk to Jubilee.

She allowed him to give her daughters horseback rides by the beach, but she hadn't stuck around for him to chat with her.

He wanted to apologize for the ride that they never got to take. He owed her that much. And he wanted to offer her a rain check, in case she wanted it. He did.

He got the feeling she was avoiding him when half of the week went by and despite the fact that he hung out at his mom's as much as he could, around the hay and the horses and the other work he had to do, he didn't get a chance to talk to her.

He found out from Clara that she often took a couple of hours after lunch to take the girls to the beach and play in the waves.

It was Wednesday before he was able to get away after lunch and walk down to the lake.

Nora hadn't apologized for her behavior, but she hadn't gone off on him about wanting him to get together with Eva again, either. His mom had told him that he should talk to Nora about it some.

He wasn't sure he could be as compassionate as what the situation demanded. She was young, and of course she wanted parents. Two of them. Like every other kid she knew. But there was no way he was getting together with Eva. He hadn't wanted to be with her to begin with. He just made a foolish decision, had given in to temptation and hormones.

He wasn't sure he was going to explain all that to his twelve-year-old, and she didn't seem overly convinced when he'd told her that he hadn't been with her mother to begin with.

But neither one of them would be happy in a relationship together at this point in their lives, and if Eva were being honest, she would admit it.

Regardless, while he didn't feel as close to Nora as they had always been, they'd gone back to taking their sunrise rides on the beach. Last year, she practiced some Roman riding, and the last two mornings, they'd worked on that as well.

He didn't particularly want her to grow up to be a trick rider, but she enjoyed testing her skills and doing things that were just a little bit dangerous. He felt like he was walking a fine line between allowing her freedom to take risks versus his natural instinct as a dad to want to protect her.

Regardless, they weren't quite back to normal as he walked down to the beach, knowing from his mom that Jubilee had taken Nora with her and her girls when she'd gone down earlier.

And she'd been doing it each day that week.

Nora usually went to his mom's to eat, and he didn't always make it. He'd been busy enough the last two days that he'd sent her on up without him.

Today, he had some fence to fix and some horses to put back again, and he got it done in time not to eat but to see Jubilee on the beach.

She had a notebook and a pen, and she sat back away from the water while the girls laughed and played and ran through the waves.

He almost didn't want to interrupt her, since it looked like she was working.

"Hey, there," he said as he walked out. Feeling like it was a little bit lame, but not knowing what else to say. Why have you been avoiding me? Sorry I was a jerk.

Neither one of those two things seemed like great things to lead off with either.

She startled, glancing up, her sunglasses firmly on her nose, a floppy-brimmed hat shading her face.

"Um. hi," she said, and she sounded a little breathless. Maybe that was just because he surprised her, but he hoped it was because...he had a little bit of an effect on her. The way she had on him.

"Is it okay if I sit down?"

He almost started to sit, but he waited for her nod before he settled down beside her. Not too close. He liked her, was interested in her, felt drawn to her, but he didn't want to push her.

"I wanted to apologize."

No point beating around the bush. If she was working on something and she didn't want to be interrupted, he at least wanted to get the apology out.

"You don't need to."

"I do. I asked you to go horseback riding with me, and then I allowed someone else to push in on it without checking with you. I shouldn't have."

"No. That's totally wrong." She closed her notebook, shoved her pen through the spiral binding, hooking it with the clasp, and set it aside before she turned to face him. "I was thinking about that, and I was afraid that you were going to feel guilty."

"I do. I should. I... It was you and me making a choice to do something, and she pushed in on what you and I had already planned. If someone else was going to be involved, I should have come to you. We should have talked about it. I should have made sure you were on board and okay."

"No. That's what I was saying. I mean, if it were a date or if we were doing a job or working together on a project or something, yeah. You definitely should have talked to me. Before we involved someone else in it, we should both agree. That's just courtesy, of course. But that was just a casual, friends doing something together, didn't have any type of meaning attached to it at all. In fact, after you told Eva she could go, I realized that I shouldn't have said yes to begin with. Because it gave the wrong idea."

"What wrong idea?" He was really just a little bit confused. She seemed to be saying that they were friends, and then he wasn't sure what she meant.

"Well, I don't want you to think that I'm open to the idea of you and me doing things together, alone. I mean, I definitely would like to take a horseback ride on the beach, but I probably should rent the horses myself and do it on my own. It shouldn't be something that you and I do alone together. That gives the total wrong impression."

"What wrong impression?" he asked, even though he suspected that he knew the answer.

"I wouldn't want people to think that we're together. That there's something going on. To see us and think that there's more. I... I came out here because I need to get my head on straight. I need to figure out my life. Not get entangled with someone else."

"You say entangled like it's a bad thing."

"It is," she said emphatically.

"But if you're looking for a new start, why can't that new start include entanglements?" he said, wanting to use finger quotes around the word "entanglements," because he didn't really think that he wanted to be considered an entanglement. After all, he looked at her as someone who made him better, not as someone who dragged him down, which is what the word entanglement implied.

"My new start needs to be me, my girls, us together taking care of ourselves. It can't involve distractions."

He didn't appreciate being considered a distraction either.

It seemed like everyone in his life wanted to try to distance themselves from him. Nora and now Jubilee.

The first woman who had caught his eye in a really long time, and she just considered him an entanglement and a distraction. He didn't even have words to try to convince her that he was anything else. And he wasn't sure he should. Except, he wanted to be more. He wanted to be part of her new start.

"I guess I was going to offer that if you wanted to go for a ride on the beach, I was still open to the idea. We could...meet at sunset and go." He wasn't even sure why he was saying that. She'd been pretty clear what she had wanted to do. Or not wanted to do.

Maybe she felt like she had too, because her lips pulled back. And she looked out toward the lake, admiring and at the same time keeping an eye on her girls.

"Well, how about we do this: you usually take evening rides anyway. If I want to go, I'll show up. How would that be?" She gave him a small smile, but it didn't reach the whole way to her eyes. It felt a little forced. Like she was just saying that to him because she didn't want to outright refuse him.

He thought that she'd been as interested in him as he had been in her. Maybe she'd been more offended than he thought because he allowed Eva to come between them. Or maybe, she really had decided that she wanted to go in a different direction and she was trying to cut him out as gently as she could.

Either way, he thought she still probably had feelings for him.

"All right. If you want to come, you'll show up." He had an idea of something he could do to force her hand, but he didn't mention it. Instead, he looked out toward the lake where the girls laughed and played. "I wanted to thank you for taking Nora out to the beach with your girls every day. Clara's been telling me that's what you've done, and I appreciate it."

"I appreciate you letting her go. She plays well with my girls, and they're thrilled to have a friend. I only wish she could stay for the school year so they'd have someone to start their new school with."

"Yeah, you and me both. It's always hard to let her go at the end of the summer."

"Yeah. I... I'm talking with my ex, back and forth about what we're going to do with our girls. He's not super interested in seeing them, but he feels like it's his duty. I think. That's the impression I'm getting anyway."

"Like he's a bad dad if he doesn't at least want to see them a little bit?"

"That, and I also think he thinks that the more time he spends with them, the less he will have to pay in child support. He already pays a very small amount, but I guess I just don't care. I would rather have them for myself than share them with him, although...after seeing Nora and how much she longs for a dad,

I guess the girls know that their dad doesn't always take time for them, but I'd like them to have the illusion that he cares a little about them and wants to spend time with them, you know?"

"It's not an illusion on my part. I'd take her full-time if I could. In fact, I've wondered if maybe I should ask Eva if I could have her for the school year and she could have her for the summer. The problem is, it's so much fun here in the summer, and I know Nora loves it here. I haven't even broached the idea with her because I think that it would make her sad, the idea that she wouldn't be spending summers with me anymore."

"Eva might be here for good. And then, she really would be by the lake in the summer. And as much time as she spends with Lana, you might have her a good bit in the summer."

He hadn't considered that. He was somewhat disquieted at the idea of Eva actually staying.

"You really think Eva is going to settle down here?" He hoped he didn't sound too horrified at the idea.

He must've sounded a little bit disgruntled though, if Jubilee's smile was anything to judge by.

"Is that such a horrifying prospect?" she asked.

He grinned back. "I'm sorry. I just... I feel like she's been chasing me a little bit, actually a lot. And she definitely put ideas in Nora's head. Ideas that I don't know if I'll ever overcome. Ideas that have made Nora look at me like I'm the bad guy. And it bothers me."

"Of course it does. I didn't mean to laugh at that."

"I know you didn't," he said easily, and this was what he liked so much about Jubilee. She was easy to talk to. She smiled, laughed, wasn't afraid to poke a little bit, but didn't make fun of him to the point where he felt defensive or hurt.

She pushed him in just the right way.

She gave a little self-depreciating laugh. "I didn't want to be unkind, but it was kind of funny the way you said it. You know her better than I do, but she just seems a little...clueless, not mean. You know?"

He supposed he understood that. "You mean, she's just so wrapped up in herself and doesn't really mean to hurt other people, just does it because she blunders around without really thinking about anyone but herself and what she wants?"

"I do that too, sometimes," Jubilee said, nodding her head.

"Maybe some of us start thinking about the way our actions affect others earlier than other people do. Seems to me that maybe Eva hasn't started thinking that way yet."

"I think sometimes it's hard for anyone to get themselves out of the center of the world and make something else, preferably Jesus, the center of their life. We... We think we do that because we read the Bible, or because we pray before we eat, or because we think about Jesus sometimes. But when you really live a life where Jesus is at the center, it's a different life than what most people live. And people can tell."

"I'm not gonna disagree with that. And I know you're talking about me. Because a lot of times, my life is all about me and what works for me. Sometimes I even think about Nora and my family. But that's not really a life putting Jesus at the center."

"No. It's not. A life with Jesus at the center is radically different. It's often uncomfortable, although sometimes the biggest blessings come from things that we think we're giving up, but instead, God just wants to divert us into something that's even better than what we left."

"You could be talking about what you're doing. Making a new life for yourself here."

"I could. I... I guess a lot of my pull toward Strawberry Sands was the fun that I had here when I was a teen. It brought back good memories, gave me a good feeling. But I do want to put my girls first and do my best by them. I suppose that is my focus. What I can do for them."

"And that's why no entanglements?" He couldn't help but ask. The idea had nagged at the back of his head the whole time they'd been talking.

She pulled her legs up and wrapped her arms around them.

"You disagree with me." She stated that as a fact; she wasn't asking. She didn't look at him either, but lifted her head to the breeze, and allowed it to push her hair back over her shoulders. She closed her eyes, as though enjoying the touch of it on her face, and he couldn't help but look at her, watch how she enjoyed the simple thing of the sun on her face and the breeze blowing gently, the sounds of the girls laughing and the waves, and the lazy summer afternoon. It wasn't even a whole day. She'd worked hard all morning and had an afternoon of hard work ahead of her. She was just enjoying the moment as it came, allowing him to share it with her.

Couldn't she see that spending her life with someone was better than spending it alone?

Of course, he'd spent the last decade or so being very content all by himself. Just visiting his family when he got a little lonely, content in his cottage, sharing it with his daughter over the summer.

He couldn't fault Jubilee for feeling the same way. Maybe it would take a while before she was ready to want to be with someone again.

The thought discouraged him, because he felt like he was ready now.

"I do. I think that the girls would bene-fit from having a father. Someone who cares about them. After all, God didn't want a child to grow up in a home with-out a mom and a dad both."

"Well, I definitely can't argue with that. Because it's true. God wanted a child to have a mom and dad. That was His plan. But because of sin, because of the fall, His plan isn't always carried out the way He wants it to be. But I shouldn't just go marry the first guy who will have me just because I want my girls to have a dad. Right?"

"Of course. I didn't suggest that, did I?" He didn't want that at all. He wanted her to consider him. Not to marry. He cer-tainly wasn't ready for marriage. Wasn't even thinking... Well, what else would he be thinking? Just to have an endless, casual, little more than casual, maybe we'll do something eventually kind of relationship?

Of course he should be thinking about marriage. What other reason would there be to have a relationship? Just to spend time with someone he enjoyed? That would be friendship. Friendship with any kind of "benefits," for lack of a better word, would mean that he was thinking about a marriage relationship.

He definitely wanted more than friendship with Jubilee. He didn't daydream about his friends. Didn't wonder what they were doing all day. Didn't lie down in his bed at night and wish they were with him.

For sure, Jubilee was not someone he was looking at in a friend kind of way.

But he could hardly admit that to her. Not now.

He laughed a humorless laugh at himself. She had to know it. Why else would he be down here on the beach sitting with her? Why would he have apologized and still want to go riding with her? She knew it, and she was telling him she wasn't interested.

He felt dense.

"I guess I owe you another apology," he said, getting ready to push himself off the sand.

"Why?" she asked, opening her eyes and looking at him, confusion on her face.

"Because you were clear. You aren't interested in me. And here I am, sitting with you trying to talk you into it. That's not exactly considerate. When you said no, I should have left."

He was going to push himself up, but her mouth dropped, and her brows drew down like she disagreed with him.

Her expression was enough to make him pause to listen to what she was going to say.

"You don't owe me an apology. I... I guess I could be wrong. If... If there was someone with whom I would like to have an entanglement with," she smiled a little at that word like she knew it had been bothering him, "it would be you. You are caring and concerned about your daughter, kind to people, not afraid to apologize, which honestly is a huge deal. I can count on one hand, with no fingers, the number of times my ex apologized to me. That is honestly more impressive than anything. Although, I suppose an apology without a behavior change isn't really worth much."

"I guess that was my cue to leave."

"No. It wasn't. I was just thinking that maybe my ex has apologized to me at times, but it's more a belligerent, I'm sorry that you have a big problem with it, that's too bad for you, and then he just continues to do whatever he wants to. Anyway." She laughed a little. "Maybe I'm a little confused. I want to do the right thing, you know? I don't want to get into another marriage where my girls and I aren't important, where we're not loved and cared for." She sighed. "I don't want to say happy. Because that's not really what I mean. Maybe I don't want to be in another relationship where it's not important to be a family. Where I'm the only one who's interested in having a relationship, and I'm the only one who tries to do things to build our relationship and make our family strong. Does that make sense?"

"Your ex was a jerk, and you don't want to end up tied to another jerk."

"I'm aiming a little higher than 'not a jer k.'"

He laughed, and she joined him. He liked that they could share some easy laughter, share some deeper conversation, that it wasn't just surface information.

"Of course you are."

"And you definitely fit that bill anyway. No apology necessary, and I'm sorry if I am giving a lot of mixed signals. I guess that's just what I was saying. I don't really know what I want, or what's going to happen, or what the best thing to do is. I just know right now, I need a job, need to make money, need to figure out where I can live, and I need to make sure that I can support my girls. Those are my priorities for right now."

"And they're good priorities. How about this, we'll just be friends who ride horses together sometimes."

"Sometimes?" She laughed. "And sit on the beach together, and talk about everything and nothing, while our girls play in the lake."

"We're just parents watching our kids play."

"Exactly."

He had settled back down and was ready to stay for a while, but she looked at her watch.

"I better be getting back. Your mom has been so good to me, and I don't want to take advantage of her. She really has a heart to help and serve and love people."

"I see a lot of her in you."

She paused as she gathered up her notebook and pen, and tilted her head, looking at him. "That's about the best compliment anyone could give me. The more time I spend with your mom, the more I admire her and hope that I might be just a little bit like her someday."

"You're on your way."

He pushed to his feet, then held his hand out for her. He almost thought she wasn't going to take it, as she looked at it for what felt like a very long moment before she put her hand in his and pulled herself up.

"Thanks. Thanks for the talking, the conversation, and the laughter, and for not thinking I'm completely crazy."

"I think we all have a little bit of crazy in us."

"Some of us have a little more than others," she said, and he had to admit she was probably right about that.

Chapter 17

"When I was at the diner earlier today, Griff gave me this to take to Kim and Davis." Lana pointed to two big pieces of cheesecake on a plate wrapped in plastic wrap. "He said they hadn't been to the diner to try it, and he was hoping that we could send it on down. Knowing Griff, it was just something he wanted to do since they got home from the hospital and to celebrate their marriage."

"Will he come to their celebration on Saturday?" Jubilee asked as she looked at the wrapped pieces of strawberry cheesecake. They were so delicious. They made her want to go back to the diner.

"I don't know. He might. When he goes to church, he kinda hangs out in the back, not that he is antisocial, he just...doesn't seem to feel comfortable in a crowd."

"I can understand that."

"Would you mind taking it down?" Lana said, like Jubilee would turn down any request she made of her. Jubilee couldn't imagine Lana asking her to do anything that she would refuse. After Lana had taken her under her wing, Jubilee felt like she owed her so much more than she could ever repay.

Today, Friday, she'd gotten her first paycheck. It had been far more than what she was expecting and more than she felt she deserved, especially since she was taking up two whole rooms in the bed-and-breakfast. She had thanked Lana profusely and assured her that she was looking for a place to stay, but Lana had brushed that off and told her that she and her girls were welcome to stay as long as she wanted.

Jubilee wasn't quite sure how Lana was going to make a profit with her taking up so much space, but she didn't say anything, just did her best to take as much of the load off Lana as she could.

"I don't mind at all."

"All right. I promised the girls that we'd sit out on the deck and I'd do something fun with them."

"I'm sure they're looking forward to that."

Jubilee had barely said that when Nora burst in the front door. "Dad is here, and he wants to know if you'll go for a horse ride with him?"

Jubilee glanced up. "Your dad is here?"

Nora nodded. "He's riding a horse and leading Bucket. He wants you to go with him. He sent me in to ask."

Jubilee had to take a moment to gather her wits about her. Although, a part of her brain registered the fact that

Nora's relationship with her dad seemed to be restored. Teens could be so up and down. But she was grateful for that much at least. After all, she knew how much it meant to Matt.

"You go on ahead. You've been wanting to go for a while, and he's got the horse here," Lana said as she stood, getting a plate of cookies she'd made that afternoon off the shelf and setting them down for Nora to grab a couple.

"Are you sure?"

"I'm sure. We're going to be busy next week, because we're booked solid, so enjoy a little bit of free time while you have it. Plus, evenings are your time."

That's what they decided. Since she was getting up early and helping to cook the breakfast that was offered as a part of everyone's booking.

Most people had checked out by noon, although they had people who stayed three or four nights, and they offered a casual buffet-type supper for a small fee.

Jubilee helped prepare that, and she also helped clean up.

"Hurry up. He's waiting," Nora said, her mouth full of cookie.

"Come on. Let's go out to the back-yard, where Penelope and Scarlett are. They've been hoping you'd come."

"Really?" Nora said, shoving the rest of the cookie in her mouth.

Lana glanced over her shoulder before they disappeared out the door.

Jubilee still stood in the middle of the room. She hadn't been planning on going anywhere, but...she had to admit that part of her wanted to. A big part of her remembered what they said about being friends and all that. And she smiled a little as she remembered that she told Matt that maybe she'd show up.

It was just like Matt to take things into his own hands. She supposed she should be irritated, but it made her smile, because that was the kind of person Matt was. He didn't sit around and wait for other people to act, but he moved himself.

She liked that about him for sure.

Deciding she didn't want to keep him waiting any longer, she resisted the urge to take a look at herself in the mirror over the buffet as she walked through the dining room and to the front door.

She opened it and then couldn't help but laugh. Matt indeed was on Boots, and he had Bucket saddled and bridled and waiting behind him. He sat in Boots's saddle, watching the door.

When she opened it, a big grin split across his face, and maybe she was imagining it, but he looked relieved.

"I wasn't sure whether you would come or not," he said, giving her a smile before dismounting.

"I thought we agreed that if I wanted to go for a ride, I would walk down to the stable?" She couldn't help but give him a hard time about it. Even though she appreciated him taking the initiative. If he hadn't, she probably never would have walked down. And she would always have wished she had.

"You know, I think there is a time for a man to sit back and let someone else do things, but there's also a time where a man needs to step up and get things done himself. This felt like one of those times. I could be wrong, but I'd be willing to bet that if I were sitting around waiting for you to come to me, I'd be waiting for a really long time."

She lifted her shoulder but grinned and nodded in acknowledgment.

As she was walking down the walk, movement caught her eye.

"This is about the fourth or fifth time I've seen that dog walking the streets. Have you seen it?" She nodded toward the Great Pyrenees that she'd seen several times and just forgot to ask anyone about. He always seemed like he was...making his rounds of the town or something. He didn't wear a collar, and while he didn't seem wild and definitely didn't seem dangerous, he didn't seem to have an owner either. Although he walked with purpose.

"I've seen him too. And I guess I just assumed that it was someone's dog who got out. The fact that he's not running away or bothering anyone, I guess it didn't seem like an emergency and slipped my mind."

"Me too."

"He just seems like he knows what he's doing."

"I think that's a quality of Great Pyrenees. They have a tendency to make the rounds of their flocks since they were bred to be guardian dogs. I believe that's the breed that I've heard is really hard to keep in, if you just have a small property. Because they want to protect their flock."

"Interesting. I guess I don't really know anything about them, but he just looked so serious. It makes sense to me that he would look serious if it's his job to protect someone's animals. That's a pretty heavy responsibility." There was humor in Matt's voice, and she glanced at him. He was grinning.

"You're not concerned about it?" she asked. In her mind, she had been going over whether or not they should catch it, maybe take its picture and put it up on the streetlights. Except Strawberry Sands wasn't that big.

"Not really. I think I've seen it the most around Davis and Kim. And I actually did ask them. They said they didn't know who he belonged to, but that they had been putting food out for him. Which he has been eating. Davis knows the vet down the beach a bit, and he was going to ask about a rabies shot, if they didn't have any takers on someone claiming him. They said they talked to Griff and Chi at the diner."

"I guess that's the place to go if you want to get news around Strawberry Sands," she said, having reached the gate and stepped through it. She looked at the horse. It had been a long, long time since she'd been on the back of one. "Maybe I should just pet him for today."

Matt laughed. "You can certainly pet him, but you are going to look kind of weird leading him instead of riding him, especially if I'm riding Boots. I promise, he is the gentlest horse I have. I chose him deliberately because I wasn't sure how long it'd been since you'd ridden. You said you had some when you were younger."

"A lot younger," she said, thinking how many years had gone by and how much she'd forgotten.

"Can I admit I'm a little bit scared?" she finally asked as she put her hand on the sleek neck of the dark brown horse. His mane was black, and she thought that he would be considered a buckskin. Either that or a bay. She couldn't quite remember what the difference was. At one time, she would have been able to say. She had loved horses from the time she was old enough to know what they were. But it wasn't something that she'd been able to be around much in her life.

You could be now.

The thought came out of nowhere. She blinked. Thinking. That was true. Matt had definitely shown an interest in her. The fact that he brought horses up without her having to ask, and the fact that he sought her out on the beach, wanted to be with her even when she stiff-armed him, made her think that he would be open for more. And a relationship with Matt would almost assuredly mean she could ride horses whenever she wanted to.

So could her daughters. They'd loved the little bit of riding that they'd done, and they begged for more.

She tried to put those thoughts aside. If the Lord wanted her to be with Matt, He was going to have to show her very clearly. After all, she'd decided that she was here in Strawberry Sands to get her life together, and while Matt had some good thoughts about perhaps God wanting her to get her life together by getting together with him, she wasn't completely sold on the idea.

Not because of Matt, but because of her. And her girls.

She took a deep breath. "All right. I know I need to do this, I want to. It's…going to be a beautiful sunset tonight, I think." She lifted her gaze up toward the lake, where the sun was just now lowering over the horizon. Matt had perfect timing.

"I can give you a hand if you want me to," he said, wrapping the ends of his reins around the fence before letting go of Boots and just holding onto Bucket.

"I'll take you up on that. It looks like a long way up, and it'll probably look like an even longer way down."

"We'll just be walking, and I can lead your horse if you want me to."

He was being so solicitous, and she appreciated it. But she didn't want to be a baby. "I'll take you up on that if I have to."

She took a minute more to admire Bucket. He was such a beautiful horse. His mane and tail flowed in the late breeze, and his coat shone with health.

"All right. I'll put my left foot in the stirrup, and I'm going to hold onto the saddle horn, and hopefully I'm still able to lift myself up."

"You can do it. I have faith in you."

She laughed a little, because she thought maybe his faith was misplaced, but she hoped it wasn't.

Bucket didn't move at all when she put her left foot in the stirrup, then gave a jump as high as she could with her right foot, pushing up with her left and trying to straighten it as she swung her right leg over.

To her surprise, she made it up on the first try. It wasn't exactly graceful, but she was in the saddle.

She remembered to keep her heels down, her toes out, as she settled into the saddle.

"He doesn't really respond to leg cues at all, so you don't have to worry too much about that," Matt reassured her.

"I didn't take lessons long enough to know too much about leg cues other than that there are some. I think if Bucket isn't one of the super deluxe models that do everything, he and I will probably get along just fine."

"I like that. Super deluxe models. I don't really have any of those. Boots is probably the closest thing I have, and he's nothing truly special. The horses that we get for renting out, we get more for safety and for responsiveness to riders. After all, I can't determine what kind of experience anyone will have when they rent from us. So I need a horse that's going to respond to anything. And not need to be treated with kid gloves."

"That makes sense. I guess it's all those things you never think about when the business isn't yours."

"True. When you don't have the experience, it's kind of hard to imagine what everything might entail. That's why it's fun to talk to people and find things out that you don't know. Expand your circle, so to speak."

"Good point." She had definitely expanded her circle by coming to Strawberry Sands. "Living with Lana, your mom, has shown me what kind of mom I want to be. I didn't have that experience growing up, and I didn't really have that idea in my head, the idea of being happy and teaching my children to be happy too. Teaching them to enjoy working, and letting them know that work doesn't have to be drudgery. If we have the right attitude about it, it's fun."

He nodded, and she realized she had been rambling a little bit. Probably because she was nervous.

"Bucket can probably tell that he is making me nervous, but I think you can hand me the reins. If he runs away, he can't go any further than the lake."

"That's true, although he can swerve and ride up the beach a pretty good ways. But it's not like he's going to run into any obstacles, and as long as you hang on, you'll probably be able to ride it out until he gets tired."

"That's the wrong answer."

"What?" He looked at her like he didn't understand what she was saying. Then he saw her smile.

"You're supposed to say that he's not going to run away with me at all, so I don't have to worry about it."

"Oh." He grinned. "He's not going to run away with you at all, so you don't have to worry about it."

She laughed, but she said, "It's too late. But at least now you know for someone else."

"Thank you. I appreciate you making sure that I know the proper answers. It's a learning experience."

He handed her the reins, watched for just a moment while she adjusted them in her hands, holding them the way she'd been taught, before he nodded almost imperceptibly and untied Boots from the fence.

Chapter 18

Matt swung easily into the saddle, like he was born into it, although Jubilee knew he wasn't. Not really. But he'd been riding for a lot longer than she had, so it made sense that he was more comfortable than she.

"You ready?"

"Yep." She didn't feel ready, but her voice didn't shake, and she was grateful for that, at least.

He turned his horse, and they walked down the street.

Strawberry Sands was not busy, not even a little, and they walked right down the middle of the street.

"I love that sound," she said as the horses' hooves clip-clopped on the macadam road.

"Me too. There's just something really relaxing about it. So rhythmic, and just a perfect sound, not too sharp, but it gives you a satisfied feeling."

"Something about horses too. They are fun to watch, majestic, noble, and are like eye candy almost."

"They're a selling point. You can put a picture of a horse pretty much anywhere, and it draws people's eyes. It's kind of like flowers, it makes people smile."

"That's true. I mean, I don't think you could probably sell toothpaste with horses, but—"

He huffed out a laugh. "I don't know. If you get the right angle, they do have nice teeth sometimes. Big anyway."

"All the better to bite you with," she said.

"Have you been bitten?" he asked casually as they got to the end of the street. There was no fanfare there, it was just where the macadam ended and the sand started, and they continued on down the dunes and to the shore.

"Several times actually. The place where I took lessons had a really great horse for beginners. She was super sweet and an absolute dream, one of those horses that you knew were never going to run away with their rider."

"Never say never," he said ominously.

"All right. That you were almost certain were never going to run away with their rider. But she had a nasty habit of biting. She got me three times, leaving bruises all three times. I wasn't exactly afraid of her, but I did learn to be very careful when I was saddling her."

"Interesting. Usually horses that are easy to ride have easygoing personalities and great barn manners too."

"She was a contradiction, I think. But the place used her because she was just such a great saddle horse."

"I suppose we all have our things."

"Have you been bitten? I mean, I'm going to assume that you have been. It's kind of hard to work around horses and not."

"Yeah. Multiple times. Never really that bad though. You talking about her leaving bruises… I don't remember ever getting bitten that bad. Although, I've had my foot stepped on more than once."

"Oh goodness. I never even thought about my flip-flops. I definitely don't have the footwear to be riding today."

"I thought about it when I saw them, but I figured it really didn't matter. Nora loves to ride bareback. And she'll be in her bare feet, bareback, and just riding with the wind."

"I love watching that. I don't think I'll ever be a good enough rider to ride bareback. I'd fall off for sure, but it's just really fun to watch."

"Yeah. She's really gotten good over the years. And she's been Roman riding this past week."

"Roman riding, that's when they stand up on the backs of the horses?"

"You have two horses together, and yeah, she'll have one foot on one and one foot on the other."

"Okay. I am not sure I understand why anyone would want to do that, but I feel like someone's dad allowed her to because he was trying to butter her up."

"I think I'm gonna have to plead guilty to that. I had told her last year, toward the end of the year, that she would be allowed to do it more this year. So I did tell her, but yeah. She was kind of mad at me for a while, because of some of the things Eva said, and that definitely helped bring her around, when I asked her if she wanted to Roman ride."

Jubilee laughed. "Sometimes as parents you have to be tricky."

"And not living with your spouse makes it hard. Especially when you're sharing custody with someone who doesn't hesitate to use your child as a pawn."

"That's sad."

They were quiet for a bit, then Jubilee thought of the issues she was having with her own ex. He hadn't responded to her texts in several days, and he probably wasn't going to. Not until it was closer to time for them to go to court. Then he would remind her that he wanted some kind of different custody agreement, if only because it would make his child support payments less.

"I was thinking about telling my ex that I don't want any child support."

"Why would you do that? Is Mom paying you that well?" he asked as a rather large wave came up, and their horses splashed through it.

Jubilee thought that Bucket and Boots both enjoyed that. Maybe the cold water felt good on their hooves.

"Your mom's been better to me than I deserve for sure. She's got a heart of gold. I think it would be easy to take advantage of her, and I hope I don't end up doing that."

"I think you were afraid of that the last time we talked, and I just want to tell you that I don't think you have to worry about it. You are not the kind of person that would naturally take advantage of people. I think your inclination to try to pull your own weight will far outweigh any desire you have to take advantage of someone."

"I hope so."

"As for telling your ex you don't want child support, why would you do that?" he asked again.

"Because I think that if I tell him that I don't want child support, I'll find out that he really doesn't want any different custody arrangement. After all, I think he does love his girls, but he doesn't really want to be bothered with them, you know? He's got his new flame, and they are expecting, and we're just kind of in the way."

She didn't mean to make it into a sob story, and she didn't mean to make it sound like it hurt, although it did. She'd been tossed away, and no matter what kind of spin she put on it, no matter how many times she told herself that she was better off without him, it still hurt.

"I think you're probably right. I mean, I don't know him or anything, but if he's trying to get out of paying, that would do the trick."

"And I think that trying to fight about custody is just going to be a pain. Partly because of what you're going through with Eva. Not that she's a terrible person or anything, but the temptation is to complain to your kids about what a terrible person your ex is. And it's easy to poison their brains. It's hard enough to raise children. You don't need the adults in their lives making it a lot harder. You know?"

"Amen and amen," he said fervently, making her smile. Since he was going through it, he would know exactly what she was saying.

And it was obvious he agreed with her.

"Sometimes I wonder why people can't just grow up, you know? Why is it so hard to put your child's welfare ahead of your own? I mean, I understand that sometimes you're bitter and angry against your spouse, but can't you see how it hurts your kids whenever you're bad-mouthing their parent? No matter how right you are, it's never beneficial." She didn't mean to rant like that, she just...felt like it wasn't that hard to figure out.

"I'm not disagreeing with you, but I know there have been a few times where Eva has been supposed to do things, and she hasn't. She hasn't kept her end of the bargain, she hasn't done what she said she was going to do, and well-inten-tioned or not, I was the one left holding the bag. I was the one left trying to explain to my child why things weren't happening the way they were supposed to. On the one hand, I always tried to make sure that Nora knew that Eva loved her. But I wasn't going to take the fall for Eva not showing up when she was supposed to. It's not my fault."

Okay. Jubilee could give him that. She hadn't had that issue yet. The only issue she had was her ex's total lack of concern and interest. And she hadn't had to explain that to her girls.

"See? That's what you were saying about not experiencing it, so not knowing. I guess you're right. I don't want to look like the bad guy, when it's my husband who is the one who's not doing what he said. So that makes sense to me."

They rode on in silence for a little bit, maybe each of them deep in thought. Jubilee, for her part, wanted to stop thinking about her ex and her divorce and all the problems associated with that. She still hadn't quite gotten over the idea that she was a divorced woman. It certainly wasn't something she ever thought was going to be a way she would describe herself, but that's where she was in her life right now.

"What's the one thing that you learned from your mistakes with Eva?" she asked after a bit. Thinking that she was divorced, but she was older and wiser. She wasn't going to make the same mistakes again.

"Don't have sex outside of marriage?" Matt said with a wry smile. "Is that not PG enough to talk about? I can tone it down a little bit."

"I'm an adult. But yeah, you can tone it down if you want to."

"Don't be alone with someone, because there's a lot of temptation involved there. Definitely don't bring them back to your room, even if they ask, and if you're going to make out with someone, don't do it on a bed."

"All mistakes you made?" she asked, although she wasn't smiling. Maybe there was a little bit of humor in her voice, because mistakes were just that. Mistakes. A person couldn't sit around and cry about them.

"Yeah. All mistakes I made. All mistakes I wish I wouldn't have made. And all things that my mom told me I shouldn't do. But you know how it is, you think you know better than your parents."

She didn't really have parents, so she didn't know that. She couldn't really remember rebelling against her aunt.

"What about you? What have you learned from your ex and your mistakes there?" he asked, and she thought he sounded like he was truly interested and not just returning the question. She liked that.

"I want to be with someone who's interested in me." There. That was one mistake. "Interested in me as a person and not just as...a body. How's that?"

"That was PG," he said with a grin.

"Well, you know what I mean. And I guess I was flattered by his attention. But looking back, it wasn't the right kind of attention. I suppose not having parents I really craved...just love. You know? But I mistook physical attraction for the deep, I want to know everything about you, and I want to love you despite your flaws kind of love. The kind of love where you actually want to spend time with someone outside of the bedroom, laughing and doing things together that both of you enjoy. Or doing things that he enjoys, and doing things that you enjoy, both of you giving a little, so that you spend time together."

"So it sounds like your love language is quality time."

"Oh my goodness. You read the love language book?"

"No. My sister Sunday read the love language book. Like, in high school. And we would sit at the supper table, and she would diagnose all of us. Maybe diagnose isn't the right word, but she'd tell us what our love language was. It got really old, but we definitely all remembered and were well-versed in love languages."

"So did she become a psychologist?" Jubilee asked with a grin.

"She should have, right?" Matt said, shaking his head.

"But she didn't?"

"No. She actually runs a dog boarding and grooming kennel."

"Maybe the Great Pyrenees is hers?"

"No. She doesn't have any dogs of her own. She says she gets her fill of them during the day, and then she goes home to her apartment, and she has cats."

"You're kidding?" Jubilee laughed.

"No. I'm not even sure she likes cats, but they were two strays that she found living outside, and she adopted them. Maybe just doing a good Samaritan thing."

"Is that in Strawberry Sands?" Jubilee asked. "I know it's a small town, but is it terrible that I've basically been to the beach and to your mom's boarding-house? And Davis and Kim's stable. And that's pretty much it."

"And the diner."

"Oh my goodness, yes. How could I forget that? The strawberry cheesecake."

"That's enough said. Man, I don't know where Griff comes up with his talent, but that cheesecake is just...there are no words."

"I totally agree."

"All right. Then it's settled, after we're done riding, we'll put the horses away, and we'll go get cheesecake."

"I feel I was suckered into that," she said, laughing.

"Are you going to turn cheesecake down?"

"Not Griff's. I've never had cheesecake better than his."

After she spoke, it seemed like they both looked out toward the western horizon, where the sun was exploding in a riot of color: oranges and reds and pinks with delicate blues and yellows along the edges.

Several long, low clouds were bejeweled with a bright orange and yellow glow that was so beautiful it was almost something Jubilee could feel.

"The sunsets are amazing."

"And they're better on horseback," Matt said, and although there was a smile in his voice, his eyes were on the horizon.

She loved that. That he didn't just take it for granted that the sunset was there. That he wanted to stop and look at it and appreciate it. That maybe he was thinking the same thing she was, that God did it just for them. Just to make them smile, to give them something beautiful to look at, something to admire and to show them His handiwork and His mastery over all creation.

The horses were both quiet as they stood, without moving, listening to the waves, watching the sky, and aware of each other, but not needing to talk to share the moment. She appreciated that too. That she could talk or not talk, and Matt was okay with both.

Finally, as the glow of the sunset faded, the wind lifted her hair, and she shivered.

"It cools down quick after the sun goes down."

"It always does. Even in the summer, the wind coming off the lake is always a little bit chilly. Which I have to admit I don't mind. After the heat of the day, it always feels good."

They turned their horses and started walking back down the beach.

"Are you okay if we stop at the stable, brush these guys down, then grab a piece of cheesecake?"

She should say no. She really should, but she didn't want to. She wanted to spend more time with him. Wanted to just enjoy being in his company, enjoy chatting with him, smiling, and talking about nothing and everything.

"I'd love to." And that was the truth.

Chapter 19

"**T**hank you so much for helping me," Kristin said to Jubilee. Jubilee nodded her head.

"Of course. It's so nice of you to bring your grandmother, the least I can do is carry some food for you."

"You make it sound like I'm a tottering old woman," Heather, Kristin's grand-mother, said.

"Gram, you are a tottering old woman." Kristin laughed.

"You don't have to make it sound that way. Are there going to be eligible men at this party? I might snatch myself up a fourth husband."

"Gram!" Kristin rolled her eyes. "Please ignore her."

"Don't ignore me. Maybe I won't be looking for an eligible man for myself, but I'll be looking for an eligible man for my granddaughter, who would make some man a wonderful wife." Heather laughed and looked over at Joyce, her friend who had moved to Strawberry Sands with her, as she rolled her wheelchair down the sidewalk.

Alma, their other friend who had moved with them as well, had gone on ahead with Lana and Jubilee's girls.

Jubilee had to admit she had been looking forward to Davis and Kim's party celebrating their wedding and their daughter coming home from the NICU, not just because she wanted to meet everyone in Strawberry Sands. But because... Matt would be there.

She'd had such a great time with him the night before when they'd ridden on the beach, watched the sunset, and then gone for cheesecake.

Her figure couldn't handle a lot of nights like that, but her heart sure could.

Or maybe it was her heart that couldn't handle it. She wasn't sure.

"Wow. They strung up lights, and is that Griff at the grill?" Kristin asked, looking over at the big man, looking adorable in a chef's apron, with a ball cap on his head backward.

He was flipping burgers on the grill and looked like he had hot dogs and maybe some steaks on as well.

"Sure looks like it. I didn't think he was coming," Jubilee said, surprised to see him. But not surprised to see him at the grill.

"I bet it made him feel more comfortable to be standing at the grill. I bet Davis asked him to cook on purpose."

"You're probably right. They probably figured he'd come if he had a job. That usually makes someone who's socially awkward feel a little bit more at home. Gives them something to do," Jubilee agreed.

"He's eligible. I don't see any wedding ring on that hand," Heather said, squinting obviously.

"Gram. Stop it," Kristin said, and there was just a hint of humor in her voice, but mostly it was very firm. There was no doubt that she definitely needed her gram to lay off.

"What? He looks like a good guy. Any man that cooks is a good man," Heather said, sounding like she was spouting off age-old wisdom.

"That is not necessarily true," Kristin disagreed. She lowered her voice. "Griff is in love with Charlotte, Chi, the lady who owns the diner."

"Oh. So you're telling me he's off-limits?" Heather said, lifting her glasses to her eyes and taking a better look. "All right. I'll mark him off my list. I'll find someone else for you though. Don't worry, Kristin. Gram's on it."

"Gram. I'm perfectly happy without a man."

"You know, it's possible to be happy by yourself," Jubilee said, trying to support her friend.

"It's not. Trust me, I'm the expert with three marriages under my belt. I've been alone, and even a bad husband is better than no husband at all."

Maybe she just hadn't had a bad enough husband. But Jubilee kept that thought to herself.

She gave Kristin a look of sympathy, but she didn't see how she could help her any more. She shrugged her shoulders, lifted her hand, and Kristin shook her head, saying that it was okay.

Heather and Joyce were arguing about whether it was better to marry a man who was older than they were or younger. Alma, who'd only been married twice, both to men who were much younger than she was, thought that her way was correct.

That was probably typical. People thought that whatever way they did things was the best way to do them.

Jubilee hoped that she wasn't that kind of person when she got older. That she would have the grace to be able to admit that just because she did it didn't make it the best.

As she was thinking that, her eyes scanned the crowd. They made their way to the table where they would put the pasta salad as her gaze caught on a familiar figure.

Matt. He was engaged in conversation with someone who looked very much like him, and Jubilee figured it must be one of his brothers.

"Now there's a handsome fella," Heather said, pointing in Matt's direction.

"Gram. Please don't," Kristin said.

"If you're talking about the dark-haired one, he's taken," Jubilee said, hoping that they weren't overheard. The very least she could do would be to defend her friend from her matchmaking gram.

"The dark-haired one? He's a handsome one," Heather said, then she cast her shrewd eyes on Jubilee. "Who is he taken by?"

"Me," she said with a grin and noted that Kristin's eyebrows shot up.

As soon as Heather looked away, Jubilee caught Kristen's gaze and winked. Kristin's mouth formed an O, and she nodded. Great. She understood that Jubilee was just trying to save her from her grandma matching her up.

"You know, maybe we should be looking for a husband for you," Jubilee said to Heather, lifting her brows at Kristin, as though asking whether that might be something that they could do to get her gram's attention off Kristin.

Kristin jumped on that immediately and pointed out the two eligible men who were semi-close to Heather in age.

The conversation went from there, and Jubilee felt like she had done her friend a favor.

"Is that her?" Luke asked, nodding his head toward Jubilee.

Jubilee stood with Kristen, who lived with her grandmother and her grandmother's two friends on Main Street in Strawberry Sands. But Luke knew Kristen, so he had to be talking about Jubilee.

"That's her," he said, trying to keep his voice sounding casual. He loved Luke, trusted him with his life, but Luke was still his little brother, and wouldn't hesitate to tease him, pick on him, and absolutely embarrass him if the opportunity arose.

The closer Matt held his cards to his chest, the better off he'd be.

"She's cute," Luke said, smirking.

"She helps mom, and she does a good job. I mean, she's really taken the burden off of mom. I think Clara might be actually thinking about opening her own store now that mom doesn't need her so much anymore."

"I know why you tried to change the subject. I wasn't born yesterday," Luke said, still smirking. "That's the girl mom said you had a thing for."

"She did not," Matt shot back. There was no way his mom would say something like that to his brother.

"Well, mom said that you took her horseback riding along the beach. She didn't have to say you had a thing for her. It was obvious you did when she said that. But, I guess I can go over and see for myself what kind of woman she is."

"Stay away from her," Matt said, and it came out a little harsher than he intended. A little more desperate. A little... Scared. He didn't know exactly where his relationship stood with Jubilee, and he didn't need his brother going and ruining everything.

"Yeah. That's exactly what I expected you to say. I definitely need to go talk to her."

"And I can talk to Kristen for you. Actually, I could talk to Kristin's gram." Everyone Strawberry Sands avoided Kristen, or more accurately, they avoided Kristen's gram. To look at Kristen, was to be attacked by Heather, and to be practically herded down the aisle with wedding bells ringing all around.

No one wanted that. So poor Kristen was a pariah in town.

"You wouldn't," Luke said, and the horror in his voice was only partially faked. "I thought you loved me."

"Thought wrong, little brother." It was Matt's turn to smirk as he put a heavy hand on Luke's shoulder. "I think we're at a draw." He grinned.

"I think you might be right. Anything to avoid Miss Heather."

Luke actually shivered, which made Matt laugh.

"You know, someday you ought to brave Kristen's gram, and get to know her. She might not be a bad person. She's cute," Matt repeated Luke's earlier words.

"If you think she's so cute, you get brave and you brave her grandma. There's no way I'll get anywhere near that old lady."

"You must be talking about Miss Heather," Davis said casually as he walked up to the brothers.

Matt held his hand out, and they shook, then Davis shook Luke's hand too.

"This is quite a spread you got here. I'm impressed with the lights and you even hired a professional chef for the grill."

"He was free. All I had to do was say that I didn't know how I was going to cook everything and mingle with my guest, and Griff offered."

"Really?" Matt had to admit he was surprised. Although, he figured he shouldn't be. He would have agreed to help immediately if he knew that Davis needed something, but the idea of Griff offering hadn't entered his mind. But it made sense now.

Especially since every time Matt looked at Griff, he saw him eyeing Charlotte. Griff probably wanted to come so he could keep an eye on her. If the rumors were right, the man had a thing for her.

Thing or not, the fellow knew how to make cheesecake anyway.

"I was keeping an eye out for the girl that works in your stable. Her and her brother. I thought they'd be here," Matt said, looking around once more. He'd wanted to introduce her to Nora. The girl seemed like she might be a little bit younger than Nora, but he thought they might have horses in common. Jubilee's girls would probably enjoy talking to her as well.

"You know, there's something going on with her. I've been pressing her on where she lives. She's been kind of evading me, and I finally told her that I needed her information so that I could put her on payroll and do her taxes."

"Did she give it to you?" Matt asked, thinking from the way Davis was talking that she didn't, and he'd found out something about her.

"She did. But I checked out the address, because I wanted to talk to her parents. It's weird that she's been working for me now for almost a month, and the only person I've seen with her has been her brother. There is no telephone number, and the address was bogus."

"She gave you a bogus address?" Luke asked, incredulously. "Did you fire her?"

"No way. In fact, I was kind of afraid to press her harder than what I have. I'm afraid she'll quit."

"And you think she might have given you a bogus address because… She doesn't have one?" Matt couldn't figure out why else she would. Or what could be going on.

"I don't know. Kim and I talked about it. We said maybe she didn't have one, but could she really be homeless? At her age? Plus there's that boy that comes with her. Sometimes. Rodney. But I haven't gotten to talk to him very much either. Somehow, when I get one of them corner, the other would make a ruckus somewhere that allows the one I cornered to escape."

Davis braced his legs and shoved a hand in his pocket. His eyes followed his wife, who held their baby, and showed her off to a group of ladies.

"Kim and I thought maybe she was just embarrassed about where she lives. You know, there's a few poorer hous-es around Strawberry Sands. It's not a very well-to-do area, and maybe she just didn't want us to see how poor she was. But, the fact that I can't get her cornered. I can't get her brother cornered, and she just seems a little… shady. Distrustful. I'm not sure, but I get the feeling that if I push her too hard, she'll be gone. And I'm afraid this job might be the only reason she's able to eat."

"I heard she goes into the diner and by herself once in a while. That seems odd for a kid that old, but Griff might know more," Luke offered, his brows drawn down.

"Yeah. I'd like to get it figured out, but I don't really want her to know that I'm trying. Again, I don't want her to slip away. If she needs help, I want to give it to her with causing her to run and potentially end up in a worse situation."

"She does seem a little streetsmart, now that you mention it," Matt said. "And you're right, she's elusive. I agree with you. She seems like the kind of kid that would disappear without a trace."

"I'm not entirely sure that the kid that's with her is her brother, either," Davis said, and that honestly shocked Matt.

"It didn't even occur to me to question that."

"You're too trusting, bro." Luke laughed.

Matt supposed it was true. He'd worked on the farm all of his life, and the things he'd learned and knew were a lot different from Davis who'd been in business all his life.

It wasn't that he knew less, it was just that the things that he knew were different.

"I'm going to get to the bottom of it. I haven't wanted to pressure my wife about it too much, considering all she's been through in the last few months."

Davis grinned, but it was a grin that held a world of experience. Matt didn't doubt for a second that Davis knew what he was talking about.

Matt also did not fail to notice the pride with which Davis said the words "my wife." He wouldn't have given a thought to it just a few months ago, but after the time he'd spent with Jubilee, he supposed he had been thinking more and more about a wife himself. An older couple walked over, and they didn't get to continue their conversation as Davis introduced his wife's mother and father.

Matt had seen them around town, but he hadn't remembered their names.

He chatted for a bit, but then he and Luke just excused themselves.

"If you want to go talk to your girl, you're going to have to brave Miss Heather. I love you, dude, but you're doing that on your own. I'm going to go get me some chow." Luke slapped him on the back, then strode away with a smirk.

Matt barely watched him go, because it was hard for him to take his eyes off Jubilee.

It wasn't that she was so beautiful, necessarily. Although he found her compelling. It was just... He seemed drawn to her. Like his whole soul longed for her, and couldn't be around her without wanting to be beside her.

He supposed if they ever got together that was a feeling that would wear off, or maybe it wouldn't. Maybe that was the kind of feeling that a person nurtured into what constituted a good relationship. After all, a person could keep themselves from being ruled by their feelings.

He didn't have to want something in order to do it. If he were to ever get together with Jubilee, he would want that feeling to continue. That desire to be close to her, watch her, just enjoy looking at her.

Shaking his head at thoughts that at one point in his life he would never have considered thinking, he took a breath, fortifying himself at the onslaught he knew was about to encounter when he met up with Miss Heather, and pointed his steps in that direction.

Actually, Miss Heather might just play into his desires. After all, if he were looking at Jubilee, Miss Heather might try to get them together. Although, it was more likely she would try to match him up with her granddaughter Kristin.

Not that there was anything wrong with Kristen, she was a nice girl, but… She wasn't Jubilee.

"Good evening ladies," he said as he reached their group.

Jubilee turned her head, surprise in her eyes, and if he wasn't mistaken, a little bit of panic there too. He couldn't imagine what would cause that, and wondered if maybe he shouldn't have walked over. Maybe she was afraid of Miss Heather.

Whatever caused it, the expression didn't stay. It was replaced by a true smile of happiness. At least, he wanted to believe it was a true smile.

His was real.

The other ladies greeted him, but he had a hard time looking anywhere except for Jubilee.

"It's a pretty night," she said softly after he murmured greetings to the other ladies.

He nodded and opened his mouth to reply, but before he could, Miss Heather said, "I thought you said you two were together?" She sidled up to Jubilee, all four foot of her, and studied Jubilee, her brows drawn.

Jubilee looked like a mouse that had gotten caught in a trap. Panicked, and not knowing which direction to run.

It took Matt a few minutes moments to realize what Ms. Heather said, and what she was accusing Jubilee of.

Matt wanted to laugh, but he was also curious as to what would have made Jubilee talk like that. Still, the most important thing was backing Jubilee up. No matter what she said, he was behind her.

"We are," he said, taking the step and a half that closed the distance between Jubilee and him, as he slid his arm around her back.

To his surprise, she leaned into him, looking up at him with a smile that held more than a little bit of relief and gratefulness.

He lifted one brow at her, just for a second, and hopefully she understood that that meant that he wanted the entire story the second they got away from Miss Heather.

"I think we were just talking about maybe not making a big deal about it tonight so that we wouldn't take the attention away from Davis and Kim. This is their evening to celebrate," he said, hoping he was getting things right.

More relief flooded Jubilee's face as she nodded.

"Where is that brother of yours?" Miss Heather said, not even stopping to congratulate them on their relationship. Which, he understood. She was single-minded in her determination to get Kristin married.

"Gram. Would you please?" Kristin said, putting her hand under her Gram's elbow and tugging, looking embarrassed, as her cheeks reddened and her eyes held apologies to both Matt and Jubilee.

"If I want to see you married before I fall into my grave, I need to make sure I get it done, since you are obviously putting no effort into the situation."

"Gram. I told you. I'm happy without a man. Not everyone needs to be married to be happy."

Kristin tugged gently on Gram's elbow, and, with a last glance at Matt and Jubilee, Miss Heather allowed herself to be led away.

Kristin looked over her head, another apology on her face, which Matt shook his head about. He wanted to tell her not to worry about it.

Chapter 21

"I feel so bad for Kristen sometimes," Jubilee said softly.

"Yeah. I think she and Luke would actually-ly be pretty good together, but he won't have anything to do with her Gram. She scares him."

"That's funny. She's four feet tall and Luke must be six at least."

"Something like that," he said, really not caring how tall his brother was. That certainly wasn't what Matt wanted to talk to Jubilee about.

"So what's this about you and me? What did you tell Miss Heather?"

Jubilee blew out a breath, her eyes scanning the crowd until they landed on her daughters who were with Matt's mom. Some tension drained out of her; he could feel it under his hand which still rested on the small of her back.

He didn't want to take it away.

Her look was sheepish as she glanced up at him. "I want to say that I was helping Kristin. You know how Miss Heather is. She was scanning the crowd, trying to find men to push on her granddaughter. She landed on you, and... I want to say that I was trying to take the pressure off of Kristin by saying that you were taken, but —"

She looked away. Her shoulders went up, like she was straightening them to do something hard. "But I hated the way the idea of Miss Heather pushing Kristin on you felt. I… Didn't want that."

Matt's chest expanded. He was pretty sure that Jubilee was telling him that she was jealous. That she didn't want some other woman to have him. That she couldn't stand to see Miss Heather trying to get Kristin and him together.

"I think that means you like me."

"Of course I like you. How could I not?" Jubilee said, turning and looking at him. Her cheeks were still pink, and her eyes shone in the glow of the setting sun.

How could he have thought she wasn't beautiful? She was more beautiful to him than anyone he had ever seen.

"You've been so kind to me. You helped me any time I've needed it. Yet you don't make me feel like I'm a charity case. You make me laugh, and... There's just something about you."

"Are you trying to say you're attracted to me?" He shouldn't be teasing her. She was telling him how she felt, but she had just made him so happy, he wanted to laugh.

"Is that what it is?" She tilted her head and looked at him, and he might've thought with another woman that she was being coy. But he thought Jubilee probably really didn't know.

"That's what I would term it. That's how I feel about you anyway. That's a physical thing, but I admire your grit and your determination and your caring concern with the girls. I... I was married to someone who really didn't have that kind of care and concern."

"Yeah." She bit her lip.

"What?" He didn't mean to bring Eva into the conversation if that bothered her.

"I don't mean to change the subject." She gave him an apologetic smile. "But talking about Eva reminded me that I needed to say something to her. She and I are both responsible for the entertainment for the strawberry festival in two weeks. I have been working on getting everything set up on my end, but I haven't had a chance to talk to her. I think she's going to do what she said, but I just thought we'd communicate a little more."

"Eva can be a little slippery at times. She says that she's going to do things, and then she doesn't."

He hated to say that, because he didn't want Jubilee to worry, and he actually wanted to talk more about what they were already talking about. How she felt about him for one.

But this was important to her, and if he was truly...falling in love with her as he suspected he was, what was important to her should be important to him as well. It was one of those things that even if he didn't feel it, he would act it, just because that was what a man did for the woman…he loved.

"If you hear anything from her, I can… Do what she is supposed to do if she's not." He didn't know what else to offer.

That made Jubilee's lips pulled back, and she looked up at him like he was her hero. He loved that look, wanted to stare into her eyes all night while she looked at him like that. He couldn't even describe the way it made him feel.

"Thank you so much. You did ease some of my burden. Not that I feel responsible for Eva's jobs, exactly, it's just that if it doesn't get done, it's not just her. Since both of us are on the committee."

"I know. It's your name on the line too. Kind of the way it is in college when you're doing a paper together. There might be five people on your team, but you end up doing all the work so you get a good grade."

She laughed. "I guess that's the way it is anytime there's more than one person doing something."

Her voice trailed off a little, and then she said, "That's the way marriage could be, right? One person puts all the effort into keeping it together, and it's not really a relationship, it's just that one person holding on, unwilling to quit."

"Sometimes that's what you have to do in order to make a life for your children."

She nodded. He had the feeling that if her husband hadn't left her, she would still be with him, just for the children.

Because what child wants to be shuffled between two homes and remember that as their childhood? They wanted a home that grounded them. A mom and a dad. A child was programmed to have and need both. In the same home.

He hated that wasn't the childhood Nora had. He wished he could do something about it.

If he had the chance to go back and do it over, would he have married Eva just to try to give Nora that stable childhood?

He didn't think so. In fact, he was almost sure he wouldn't, because he was pretty sure that Eva wouldn't have stayed with him. She wasn't the kind of person who kept her word.

"I was going to ask your sister Clara if she wanted to do a booth with her artword. I've been putting it off because I know she's busy with her job, but she's right there. Do you want to come with me?" Jubilee tilted her head and looked up at him.

He grinned. After what she'd said to them, maybe she didn't realize the way it had affected him, but he felt like he'd follow her anywhere. Wanted to, in fact.

"Sure. Do you need me to help try to convince her?"

"I don't want her to do it if she doesn't want to, but I've saved a really good spot for her, and I know she's torn between whether she wants to keep her job and move to The Cities or whether she wants to stay here in Strawberry Sands. I thought having a booth at the strawberry festival might help her make up her mind."

He hadn't realized all that about his sister. He knew she liked to draw, and he would've considered her the artist of the family, but he didn't realize that she was quite as serious about it as what Jubilee was saying.

He appreciated that about Jubilee, that she paid attention to people and noticed them. He supposed he had a tendency to just focus on what he was doing and put himself at the center of his world.

Jubilee seemed to make a conscious effort to put others at the center of hers.

What a great example.

"Of course," he said as they turned and started walking toward Clara. His hand fell off the small of her back, which he hated, but as it fell, it brushed her hand which was by her side.

She didn't jerk it away, and, maybe he was being a little bold, but he allowed their hands to brush again, and then he deliberately entwined his fingers with hers.

They walked the first step just like that, before she lifted her head and looked at him.

"Is this okay?" he asked. Maybe he should have asked before he didn't, but he suspected after what she said that she might be okay with it.

"It scares me." That was all she said, but the words went down hard on him.

"I don't want you to be afraid of me."

"Not of you. Just of...doing this again." She lifted her brows, as though asking if he understood what she was saying.

He supposed he kind of did. Maybe that was why it took him so long to feel serious about anyone since Eva. He hadn't even been serious about Eva, but the repercussions had been so unexpected, and so life-changing, that he hadn't wanted to make that mistake again.

"I think I might understand. I... I'm not afraid. This feels right to me. But, I've had a lot more time since my last... I wouldn't even call it a relationship. But, since my life changed, and I realized that being with someone doesn't just affect me."

She nodded. "I have two girls to think about." Her lips flattened. "And you have Nora."

Her eyes scanned the crowd, as though she were looking for their children.

"You think they'll have a problem with this?" he asked, squeezing her hand to let her know that was what he was talking about.

"I don't think so. They adore you. I just... I don't want to fail again."

"It wasn't you that failed the first time. It was your lying cheating good for nothing husband who can't keep his vows. That's where the failure was. Not you."

It made him angry to hear her talk like all the things that happened were somehow her fault. He didn't know what kind of wife or mother she had been when she'd been married to Cody, but it didn't matter. It shouldn't matter. Cody should have kept his vows no matter what kind of wife or mother she was. There was no excuse for cheating. None.

Her hand tightened in his. "Thank you for saying that. Sometimes I just feel so... Worthless."

He hated hearing that. But before he could say anything she said, "I know I'm not. I know my worth is in Christ. That, because I'm a child of God, because he loves me, that's where my worth is found. Not in self-love, or in what my husband says or does about me. But, when someone constantly tells you that you're no good, that he would be better off without you, that everything was your fault, that you would never amount to anything without him, it's hard to remember, to believe, that God loves me anyway. Because, Cody pledged to love me. To cherish me. To spend his life being true to me. I just feel like somehow I did something wrong in order to keep him from doing that."

"Some people just don't know how to keep their promises. Some people say words never intending to keep them. Sometimes all people can see is themselves and what they want, and they use whatever words are necessary to try to manipulate people into doing what they want them to do, and they don't use their words to tell the truth."

They were in the middle of a party, and he hated that because he wanted to pull her to him, and then he decided, why not? They were still a good ten feet away from Clara who was deep in conversation with Sunday, one of his other sisters, when he pulled Jubilee to a stop, and tugged until she faced him.

He didn't want to let go of her hand, but he brought his other hand up and put it on her shoulder.

"It made me feel better to hear you say that your worth is in Christ. I think so often we think our worth is in what other people think of us. Or what they say about us. Or how they feel about us. And we spend our lives trying to make other people happy. Somehow thinking that will somehow make God happy too. But that's not what God is interested in. We can't control the happiness of other people. And God doesn't want us to try. Not that we can't do things to make them smile, to give them encouragement or a little joy in their soul, but God wants us to live for Him. And when we're living for Him, that joy and encouragement and those smiles we share will be a natural part of who we are. Regardless, it's not about what other people think of us. In fact, the Bible says that there are going to be people who aren't going to like us because we love Jesus. We have to get the idea out of our heads that we can please everyone. It's just not possible."

"I know." She hung her head. "I know it. It's just... Having people upset with me makes me feel so terrible. Like I'm bad. A bad person."

"And you can fight those feelings with the truth. That you make mistakes, and it's okay. You live your life, and sometimes that offends people. Not because you do anything on purpose, not because you're not kind, just because you're you. And then, there are people like your husband who make mistakes, and then want to blame everyone around them for them. Who can't own up to what they are. And in order to make themselves feel good about themselves, they have to knock everyone around them down, so they're the only ones left standing. But, he can't knock you down, because you aren't about you. You're about Jesus. And therefore, your life is about Him, and about pleasing Him, and so it doesn't matter what other people say.

"Sometimes they're right."

"True."

She took the wind out of the sails a little bit with that. But he rallied. "Sometimes things people say about us are correct, and sometimes we have to examine ourselves, and make changes. But, that doesn't affect our worth. That doesn't affect how Jesus loves us. And it doesn't affect our purpose, which is to live for Him."

"Good point. You're right. Just because someone says something to me with a grain of truth in it doesn't mean that I have to think they're right when they tell me that therefore I don't amount to anything."

"Exactly. Because, I think you're pretty awesome."

She grinned, like he'd said something funny.

"I'm serious. I... I admire you more than I've admired anyone in my life before. I feel drawn to you. I hope that's okay."

Chapter 22

Maybe that wasn't the best thing for Matt to say, but he wanted to move forward. Wanted to do more than hold Jubilee's hand, wanted to have the right to be beside her. But he supposed all of those things took time, and he couldn't just snap his fingers and have her wanting to be with him.

"I think that's what I want too. But, I think I just need a little bit of time. Not because of you, but to get used to everything. To get rid of the fear. You're so much different than Cody. So much better. In every way. But I suppose it's just going to take my head a little time to tell my heart. Or vice versa, whichever," she said with a little smile, and he laughed.

"I don't know which it is either, but I'm glad that you see. I was trying not to be offended that I was kind of getting lumped in with Cody and everything that he's done."

"No way. Not at all. You're so much different. Maybe because I'm older, and hopefully a little wiser too, it's easy for me to see that. Maybe it's hard to believe that someone like you could be interested in someone like me."

"I don't see why that would be so hard to believe. You're an amazing person, and it's an honor to be with you."

Did she think he was just saying that? Her brows tilted down a little as though she thought they were just words that he said to everyone. She didn't realize that when he said it was an honor, he meant it was an honor. Those weren't things he said lightly, to just anyone. There were plenty of people that he was friends with, and he liked them, but to say that it was an honor meant something. At least to him.

But he didn't get time to say anything, because he heard his name, and then, "Jubilee!"

There was a little bit of curiosity and interest in that word.

"You're holding hands with my brother. What's going on?" Clara, smiling and looking pleased that Jubilee was holding his hand, walked over to them.

Sunday was nowhere to be seen. He imagined that she was probably trying to find her son, who had a tendency to run off. Matt had never met a more energetic little boy.

"Well, when I grabbed it he didn't pull it away, so he's stuck." Jubilee smiled and returned the hug that Clara gave her.

"That's not how it happened at all. I took her hand. I didn't grab it, I gently slid my hand into hers and she didn't slap me, so that's where we are."

"Matt. Wow. After all these years. This is going to make our mom so happy. She just thinks the world of Jubilee, and the two of you —" Clara shivered a little, like she was just overcome with all the things she wanted to say.

But Matt could feel Jubilee panicking beside him. She already said she was scared. And the idea that Clara practically had them married…

Of course, what else would it mean when he was running around town holding her hand? Maybe to some people that didn't mean anything, but Strawberry Sands was small enough to know that it did mean something to him. It meant a lot to him. Everything. He should have known what the reaction would be. But he didn't realize it was going to scare Jubilee. Didn't realize the idea of another relationship was such a hurdle for her to get over. Of course, it was for him, but that was years ago.

"Clara, I actually wanted to talk to you about something else," Jubilee began, and Matt figured it was an attempt to politely steer the conversation from the direction it was going, into something that Jubilee felt she could handle a little better.

He waited. Wanting to help her if she needed it, but not wanting to jump in if she could do it on her own. He didn't figure she would appreciate that, al-though... Jubilee hadn't seemed like the kind of woman who got angry or offended when he tried to help.

He liked that, because he wanted to help. Wanted to step in and do things for her. That was one of the ways he showed that he cared.

He thought back to that whole love language book, which he would never have read on his own, but he supposed there were advantages to having sisters.

One of his love languages was service. He almost snorted, and in order to keep himself from any other noises that didn't go along with whatever conversation Jubilee was having, he dragged his attention back to her.

"Of course," Clara said, "What would you like to know?"

"Eva and I are in charge of the Strawberry festival entertainment, and we decided I would be responsible for getting vendors for that weekend. After you and I talked, I started to think that it might be nice to have an art vendor. We have a lot of food, drinks, ice cream, and even some arts and crafts type things, but no actual artwork. Would you have enough things that you could set up a stand?"

"Oh my goodness. I've never even considered any of that, although after you and I talked, I asked for an extension on the decision I have to make at my job. My boss gave me a month." She rolled her eyes. Matt knew from talking to her over the years that her boss was not exactly her favorite person.

"You know you always have the family safety net if things don't work out. Not that I think they're not going to, but you're young, you're not married, you don't have anyone depending on you, this is a great time for you to step out on your own."

Jubilee smiled at him like he said all the right things, and that feeling of his chest expanding and with all the good things beat strongly in his soul again. He figured he could pretty much do anything if he had Jubilee beside him looking at him like that.

"I don't think quitting my job is probably something I want to decide on the spur of the moment, but I've definitely been praying about it," Clara said giving him a thoughtful look. "But, I do think you're probably right that the festival would be a great way to put myself out there and maybe see how it goes."

"Sure. And that storefront is still available."

"The one right by the beach?"

"Yeah, that would be perfect for the diner. I suggested to Chi that she ought to move the diner from where it is now, to that spot right on the end."

"That's a great idea! They could make a back patio and have seating that overlooks the stable and the lake. It would be really pretty to have people sitting there eating, watching the horses grazing and enjoying the view of the lake."

"That's brilliant," Matt couldn't help but say. He could get into that right away. He'd enjoy going just for the great view.

"I agree. I hope she does it. Of course, Griff's cheesecake will still make me want to go to the diner anyway, but a view like that would make it pretty much perfect."

"She seemed interested. But moving the diner would be a lot of work. Plus there'd be even more work that would have to go into making that building on the end work for them."

"Maybe I'll talk to Griff. I could give them a hand."

"It's Chi, not Griff." Clara's look held a warning. Matt snapped his mouth shut. It wasn't a secret, at least not to him, that Griff had a thing for Chi. But, maybe Clara was telling him that the feeling was not mutual.

"Isn't that the lawyer?" Jubilee said and Clara turned her head to where Jubilee was looking immediately.

"That's him. What a jerk," Clara muttered.

Matt had to search, because he wasn't quite sure who they were looking for. But then he saw Eva, chatting with some dude who wore a polo shirt with a small logo in the upper left corner, along with khaki pants and shiny shoes that didn't look like they belonged on the beach.

"I guess I just never trusted those guys who look like they have to use a half a bottle of gel to get their hair to stay down. I don't know why, but it makes me wonder what else there is in their life that they're trying to hide," Clara muttered.

Jubilee's lips pressed together, but she didn't say anything else. It wasn't hard for Matt to read her expression though. She didn't like the guy. And he figured that Eva probably wasn't gaining in popularity by talking to him, because when he glanced over around and laid eyes on Shai, she was staring at the two with her heart in her eyes.

What a mess.

"You can put me down for a booth," Clara said with decisiveness, nodding her head.

"All right. I will."

"Didn't you want to talk to Eva?" Matt said after Clara and Jubilee hashed out the details and Clara hurried off to grab something to eat.

"I think I'll let it go for now," Jubilee said, taking her hand out of his. "If you don't mind, I think I better go catch up with your mom and my girls."

He was going to offer to go with her, but the way she pulled her hand away, and the way she looked made him feel that maybe she was still working through her issues, and he didn't want to push her.

But at the same time, he didn't want her to not know how he felt. After all, if they just danced around that, if she were thinking about whether she wanted to be with him or not, he didn't want her to wonder how he felt about her.

"I'm going to assume that's you leaving me. Sorry about the handholding."

"I liked it." She closed her eyes, almost as though she were trying to settle something inside of her, and needed the privacy to do so. "I really liked it. But, I think maybe I just need to…"

"Take it slow. I understand. Truly, but I want you to understand that the way I feel isn't going to change. What I want isn't going to change, and the way I act isn't going to change. I get that you've been with people who bailed on you, hurt you, and let you down. And that's not going to be me."

He meant those words with his whole heart, but he couldn't make her understand, couldn't make her see, and couldn't force her to do what he wanted her to. He could only stand there and hope that she chose him. And that she did it in a reasonable amount of time.

"You do realize that we would have three children together if we were to go through with us?"

"I'm okay with that. And I think they get along really well."

"You're right. I think they do. But three?"

"Maybe we would have four or five."

That made her head jerk up.

He almost laughed at how fast her head moved. But, he was serious. It wasn't that he wanted a boy, necessarily, although people would probably accuse him of that. It was just that... He wouldn't mind having a child with Jubilee. Didn't think that three children were too much. Wouldn't mind being a parent with her.

"We have such a blended family," she said, and she was chewing on her lip again.

"Is that going to be a problem?"

"It's not an ideal family."

"Is there anything in life that's ideal?"

"No. Of course not. Nothing in my life has turned out the way I wanted it to."

"And it's probably not going to start. But, they can't keep us from moving forward. From continuing to make the best decisions that we can. We can't just throw up our hands and say it's not going to be the best, so therefore I'm not even going to try."

"All right. You have a point, and I know you're right, but still just not sure how I feel about it. You know?"

"Why don't you take some time to think about it? No pressure here. Like I said, I am not going anywhere. And, I'm not changing."

"Thank you. Thank you for being patient with me. For not pushing me to be what you want me to be right this second. I... Honestly I feel like that's the way it's going to go, but I just need a little bit of time to get myself pointed in that direction.

This wasn't what I was expecting when I moved here."

"It wasn't what I was expecting when I saw you along the side of the road, either."

"Well, we'll have a fun story to tell everyone how we met anyway." She laughed a little. "Which involves me having no money, no gas, no hope. You're the hero in that story for sure."

"You are the heroine. Because I got to rescue you. I know about women's lib and all of that, but guy still wants to feel like a hero sometimes."

"Well then I can say, and you know it's true, you're my hero."

They grinned at each other a little, and it made him feel better. That she was coming around, and she just wanted some time. That she wasn't afraid to tell him that he was her hero. Maybe it was juvenile, but it did make him feel good, to know that she would let him rescue her. It made him feel even better to think that she needed him. Because he was starting to get the feeling that he really needed her.

<h1 style="text-align:center">Chapter 23</h1>

"That was so nice of Sunday to take the girls down to the beach," Jubilee said as she worked in the kitchen with Lana. Lana had become a dear friend, despite their age differences, and Sunday and Clara had both become almost as close.

Some days Jubilee wished she had been born into the Landry family.

But then, she wouldn't have Matt.

Whatever it was that she had with him. He texted her every day, and typically called her sometime in the evening. They'd gone on three more horseback rides, and probably would've gone on more if all of his horses hadn't been rented out the other days.

"That girl. She has her hands full with Quinn. He is about as rambunctious as any kid could be. But she lets that be her excuse not to move on with her life."

"Because she has a child?" Jubilee said, rolling out the pie dough for the quiche they were going to have for breakfast in the morning.

"Maybe it's fear. She's just... She lets the what-ifs get to her."

Jubilee didn't say anything for a moment. She let the what-ifs get to her. Or the why nots.

"You just can't let fear run your life sometimes…all the time, most of the time, we just don't know what's going to happen in the future. We can't. Yet we want to have everything planned out down to the tiniest little detail. But that's not the way God works."

"No. He wants us to walk by faith, not by sight."

"Exactly. And yet, walking by faith is a lot harder than what it sounds like. Because, we let fear dictate our choices."

She was letting fear dictate her choices. At least with Matt. She had asked him for time, and he'd happily given it to her.

Or at least it seemed like he was happy. Regardless, she wasn't quite sure where to move forward now. She was happy stuck in limbo. Although she'd like to have more with Matt, the idea of jumping into another relationship was scary enough that she was content to just sit back.

"I forgot to tell you that Eva was moving out."

"Really? I hoped I would get to see her this evening. She hasn't said anything to me about what she's doing with the festival, and it's only five days away."

"I haven't really talked to her much since we saw her with that lawyer at Davis and Kim's pardon. I think the whole town was mad at her, but I got the feeling that she was going somewhere with him."

"Really?"

That was so hard for Jubilee to comprehend. She couldn't imagine jumping from relationship to relationship and dragging her child with her.

"Is Matt going to get Nora?"

Lena snorted. "He'd take her in a heartbeat. But I don't think so. I wouldn't be surprised if he goes to court about it, but there's really not a whole lot he can do. Eva is allowed to make bad choices, and she's allowed to drag her daughter around while she does it."

Wasn't that so true? A person was allowed to make bad choices. And a lot of times those choices affected their children, and there wasn't a single thing anyone else could do about it.

Of course, on one hand that was a good thing, because Jubilee certainly had made her share of bad choices, and her children had suffered, but hopefully she'd learned from those bad decisions and was ready to start making good ones.

But she had a more pressing problem at the moment.

"She's moving out now? Like today?"

"She took boxes of stuff out of the basement and then drove away."

"I... Wonder what she's doing for the festival?"

"You can try calling her, but I got the feeling she wasn't planning on being around for it."

Jubilee tried to keep the panic from clawing up her chest. She was going to spend all of the committee's money to have a bunch of vendors and a bunch of seating and a stage, with no performances. No one scheduled to perform.

The first thing that her new hometown asked her to do, and it was going to be a miserable failure. Truly not her fault, but still, she was in charge.

"If you don't mind? Could I have Eva's number?"

She put the rolling pin down, realizing too late that her dough was rolled out lopsided and would never fit in a pie shell. When a person rolled out pie dough more than once it got tough, and she felt she'd not only ruined that, but possibly ruined the whole festival, too.

Her fingers trembled as she dialed the number that Lena gave her.

Swallowing hard, she realized her mouth was dry, and she thought about grabbing her glass of water, but she didn't move. Instead in her mind she begged Eva to pick up. To pick up and tell her that everything was just fine.

"Hello?" Eva was out of breath.

"Eva. I'm glad I caught you." Her voice sounded far more normal than she felt. "I just want to touch base about the festival."

"Oh that's right. I've been meaning to call you. I'm moving away from Strawberry Sands, and I'm not going to be able to do anything with the festival."

Jubilee took a calming breath. "That's fine. Can you just give me the contact info for the people that you've booked for Friday and Saturday night and I'll go ahead and be in touch with them myself."

"I'm sorry. I just haven't had time to book anyone. I've been busy with other things. You know, moving, hello."

"You...haven't booked anyone?" Jubilee asked after a small pause. Like, as in hadn't booked anyone. At all.

"No. Did you hear me? I've been busy. I've had things to do."

"But... But it was our job."

She wasn't so naïve as to know that some people didn't take their job seriously.

"It's just a small town festival. Nobody cares. Trust me on this," Eva said, disdain dripping from every word.

"Right." Jubilee wanted to argue. She certainly had all the facts on her side. But, if someone didn't think that was important for them to keep their word, there really wasn't any point in arguing. She couldn't win an argument like that when they weren't even starting out on the same level. Before she could win, Eva would have to admit that small towns did matter, and that if she said she was going to do something, it didn't matter what stuff came up, unless she was incapacitated in some way, she should have, at the very least, told someone and given the responsibility to someone else.

"Is that all you wanted?"

"Um. I guess. How's Nora? I haven't seen her for a day or two."

"She's fine. No need to be nosy." Eva laughed. "Did Matt have you call, thinking that maybe I would change my mind and let him have custody if you ask?"

"No!" Jubilee said quickly. She didn't want to sabotage anything Matt was trying to do by butting in, no matter how innocent. "I just care about her. She's... Great friends with my daughters, and I think she's sweet."

"She's never going to like you more than she likes me, so you can just forget about it."

"No. I wouldn't want her to!" She would never want to come between a person and their parents. The idea that she would was just...terrible.

"All right. I have to go. Have fun at your little festival," Eva said.

Nora looked at her phone, and the line had gone dead.

"She's not doing the festival. None of it. I have five days." She turned shell shocked eyes on Lena, whose expression showed surprise, and then, almost immediately, she lifted her head and gave a reassuring smile.

"We will figure something out. We have five whole days. We've got plenty of time. It's not like we have five minutes. Five minutes, I'm not sure we could work with. Five days...we got this."

Jubilee laughed. "All right. Thank you. Because I was starting to have a melt-down."

"I could see that."

"Nana! Miss Jubilee! Come watch me!" Nora burst into the house.

"Nora! I didn't even know you were here. I thought you were with your mom."

"Nope. She dumped me off because she went to go spend time with her boyfriend. Which, I don't mind at all because dad let me Roman ride. I want you guys to come see."

Lena looked at Jubilee, and then they shrugged.

"All right. Let me check the stuff in the oven, and then I have fifteen minutes," Lena said as she bustled to the oven, opening the door and peeking in.

Nora practically danced around them as they gathered their things, set a timer, and walked outside.

"If you stand here on the porch, you should be able to see me as I ride by. Okay?"

"I can see your dad down there holding your horses," Jubilee said as she walked to the edge of the porch.

"Yeah. Just a second. I'll run down. You've got to see this."

Nora took off, as Lena and Jubilee shared another smile.

"While we're waiting, I've been thinking, just in the five minutes since you told me, there is a family that does trick riding, and they also sing together. It's not stuff they do professionally, but I see them at different fairs and stuff. We can see if they have Friday night free. Maybe they'd even do trick riding one night and singing the other. Or maybe they could split it up between both?"

"Either would work. Anything would, but that sounds awesome. And I know one little girl who would absolutely love it," Jubilee said, and they shared a laugh.

By then, Nora had made it to the beach and they watched while she took the horses from her dad, getting on one, and nudging both of them into a walk, before she stood up on the back of one, and then put one foot on the other, holding the reins and standing straight up.

She looked over her shoulder toward where they were sitting and lifted a hand.

"Oh my goodness. That's enough to scare me to death," Jubilee said, a hand going to her heart.

Lena had the exact same look, with her hand also covering her heart, but she smiled. "She's so happy doing this. How could I not want her to do something she loves?"

"Even though she could get hurt?"

"Is that life? You aren't safe doing anything. And you might as well live it the way you want to, doing what God has called you to do and given you the talent for. And sure, if she gets hurt, she might wish that she could go back and do things differently, but we all have to take risks. If we don't, we just end up stuck in limbo, scared to move out. Scared to live the life that God has for us. Because we want to see the end, that everything turns out the way we want, rather than taking it by faith."

"Like what we were talking about before."

"Exactly. Like what we were talking about before."

They watched Nora for fifteen minutes before the timer went off, then they both walked back in the house, waving at Matt who stood down on the beach watching his daughter.

Jubilee continued to help Lena, but she knew she needed to talk to Matt and she knew what she needed, wanted, to say.

Sunday brought the girls home and Lena took them out on the porch for ice cream while Jubilee continued to work in the kitchen. By the time she had the kitchen cleaned up and the sun was setting, she asked Lena if she would mind watching the girls.

Lena said she would be happy to. She didn't ask where she was going, but she just gave a smile and a knowing look.

Jubilee figured she would tell her how everything went the next morning. Or, maybe Lena would hear about it from Matt. She didn't care. She just knew that she couldn't not take a chance because she was afraid. And it wasn't right for her to make a good man sit around, waiting on her to make up her mind, while she wanted everything to fall into line and for her to be able to see the end, instead of accepting by faith what she felt God had put in front of her.

Where are you?

She sent the text to Matt.

At the stable. Nora just ran into the house to take a shower. We were going to come up to mom's.

Can I come talk to you?

You're scaring me.

I don't think this will scare you.

I'll meet you halfway.

As it turned out, they met in front of the pasture, the horses grazing beside them, the sun setting behind them over the lake, and Matt smiling when he saw the look on her face.

She didn't know what she looked like, but she knew how she felt.

"You said you wanted to have more than a handholding relationship with me."

"I'm not sure I called it a handholding relationship." His voice held caution.

"I want that. I want more. I want… I want to try. I'm scared, but that doesn't matter. I don't have to not be scared in order to do things."

"That's the best thing I've heard all day." He moved closer as she stepped into his arms, wrapping hers around him, and looking out at the sun setting on the lake as they stood together.

"It's not every day that a girl gets a chance to have a man who is honest and upright, someone who she knows she can depend on, and who isn't going to let her down."

"I hope I can live up to all of that."

"I know you can." She was sure of it. She wasn't thinking that he was perfect. Of course he wasn't. Neither was she. But she knew that he wasn't going to leave her. That he'd had the same issues she had - she'd just experienced Eva's lack of dependability. Matt wasn't like that. He was the opposite.

"I don't want to look a gift horse in the mouth, exactly, but I'm wondering what changed your mind?" His hands slid up her back and tugged her closer to him. She pressed herself against him and lifted her head.

"I guess I just decided I'm going to walk by faith. There's a reason I ran out of gas and you stopped and things just went from there. I know this is the direction

God wants me to go, and even though I'm scared, I want to step out in faith." She took a breath. "It might not end the way I want - following God doesn't mean no pain or failure - but I want to do it with you."

His lips curved up before he lowered his head. She closed her eyes and tilted her face up, feeling his lips touch hers and loving the way it felt exactly right, like it was what she'd been waiting for all her life.

Her hands had threaded through his hair and her breath came in uneven pants when he lifted his head a long time later.

"I love you."

The words fell on her ears perfectly, joined by the sound of horses eating, waves breaking on shore and the glow of the sunset over it all.

"I love you, too."

He didn't respond to that. Not with words. But she wasn't going to complain because the second kiss was better than the first.

Clara stood at her booth, artwork that she'd drawn and painted over the years surrounding her. She'd probably stuffed way more things in the small space than she should have. But her art felt more like her babies and she had a hard time choosing what to bring and what to leave.

"I love this!" Chi exclaimed. "The colors are so pretty and the scene just says 'home' to me."

Clara smiled. Chi held a print that she'd done of her niece, Nora, sitting on the back of her horse facing the sunrise, her hair just lifted off her shoulders with the early morning breeze, her face lifted to the lake and the water, sparkling with the first rays of sun shining on the water, her horse's head lifted and regal, the beach deserted except for the two of them. It was one of her favorites too. And it said "home" to her as well.

"I really think you could ask a lot more for these. I'm not an art expert or anything, but the emotion this piece evokes is real and I would pay a lot more for it!" Chi dug in her purse for her credit card.

Clara had spent a lot of time figuring out how she could take payment and had managed to get pretty much everything set up so she could get paid however her customers wanted to pay her. Since she was considering making this her actual job, she figured she needed to do all the things necessary to make it a success.

"Thank you so much for this!" Chi smiled. She turned to the man beside her, who, in Clara's opinion, looked hot and bored. "What do you think? Isn't it amazing?"

The lawyer nodded, his lips barely turning up. "Let's go somewhere cooler and more comfortable. How would you feel about spending the weekend at my penthouse in Chicago?"

"I'd..." Chi's voice trailed off and Clara felt bad for her. It was obvious Chi was much more into the lawyer than he was into her. Emotionally, anyway. And Clara knew how that felt. She'd been in love with her boss for years.

She had no idea why. After all, everyone, bar none, in the office considered him a work-a-holic jerk.

"I wish I could, but I can't leave Griff to do everything alone."

"That guy can handle any knife fights that break out. Come with me." The lawyer paused. "And be sure to give him my number."

Clara was pretty sure that was a joke, but Chi didn't laugh and the lawyer didn't smile and maybe she was wrong.

Chi thanked Clara as they walked off, still talking.

Clara tapped her foot to the happy beat of the sweet harmony that drifted over on the lake breeze. The music Jubilee had hired for the evening was perfect. And even better since they'd been the ones to put on the trick riding performance that afternoon. It was a family of five siblings from farther up the lake in Raspberry Ridge. Clara had heard of them over the years, but this was the first she'd seen them perform. She'd seek them out in the future.

"Aren't they good?" Jubilee, walking beside Clara's brother, Matt, entered her booth with a big smile.

"They are! I can't believe they live so close, yet I haven't ever heard of them. What a great find!" She returned Jubilee's hug, squeezing a little tighter than strictly necessary, just because she was so happy that her brother had finally found a woman whom he loved and who would love him the way he deserved. Matt was a great guy and Clara couldn't be happier for both of them.

"Sometimes things don't work out the way we think they're going to, and often that's because God has something even better in store for us." Jubilee stepped back and put an arm around Matt again. He pulled her close and she looked up. They exchanged a knowing smile, one that couples everywhere used to communicate without words.

It made Clara's heart both happy and sad to see it. Happy because both Jubilee and Matt were so deserving of love and happiness, but sad because she couldn't seem to get herself to focus on anyone but her boss who was emotionally unavailable, and not even someone she really wanted to like, let along carry a torch for years for.

"I think Nora found some new heroes," Matt said.

"Where are your kids?" Clara asked, knowing that together they had three.

"Mom has them. You know her. We'll be lucky if we get to spend any time with them today at all. She's in her glory when she's hanging out with kids."

"I know. She's so good with them too. I've never met a child who didn't love her."

"We can't stay. Jubilee needs to go make the rounds and make sure everything is going okay. Although I'm trying to talk her into messing something up on purpose. The council has already asked her to head the entertainment committee for next year."

"I'd say congratulations, but I'm not sure whether I ought to offer my condolences instead."

They laughed. "Matt's going to help me, and people have been asking to have the Grassley family back, so it might end up being easier than this year."

"Practice makes perfect."

"If you have a chance, you should try out Griff's strawberry shortcake. He's selling it at the empty building where Chi and he are thinking of moving to and it is uh-maz-ing!" Jubilee's eyes glowed.

"She knows what she's talking about. She's already had two servings of it."

"You had three!"

The look Matt and Jubilee shared made Clara's heart flip. So precious and beautiful.

Her phone buzzed.

"We'll let you go!" Matt said, glancing at her phone, then keeping his arm around Jubilee as they walked out of the tent.

Clara had a feeling she knew who was calling on a Saturday morning, and sure enough, when she pulled her phone out of her pocket, it was her boss, Alexander Hudson.

She laughed to herself because she didn't even consider not answering, even though she was thinking very strongly of quitting, and even though it was a Saturday and she was not required to work on Saturdays.

She swallowed, then swiped her phone and said, "Hello?"

"Are you coming out to The Cities?"

He called her on a Saturday just to ask that?

"I thought I had until the middle of July to decide." She really wanted to start her own art business and summer was the time. The only thing that held her back was…not seeing Alexander any more. Which was pathetic.

"I've changed my mind."

Her heart dropped. He was going to fire her!

"We're both going to work remotely from that little town you want to stay in. What's it called? Strawberry Pie Place or something?"

"Strawberry Sands. It's a lakeside town." She paused with her mouth open. "You're moving here?"

"Yes. I can work remotely. As long as they have good internet and I will make sure they do. I'll have everything set up in two weeks. Send me the directions. I'll drive in tonight and we'll have a meeting to hash everything out. Best place to set up shop. The staff you'll need to hire. Office equipment you'll need to purchase and job duties. We'll end up traveling a lot together as we'll need to go to The Cities at least once per month for in-person meetings."

"Tonight?"

"Yes."

"It's Saturday."

"You're right. I'll buy you dinner. There is someplace to eat there, right? Then we'll talk."

"Um...I have a stand...at the...Strawberry festival." She could just picture him laughing at that. So countrified and she'd never felt more like a hick than she did at that moment. She hated that he could make her feel that way, even while she acknowledged that he couldn't "make" her feel any specific way. It was all in her head.

"Fine. We'll meet there. Text me directions."

Her phone shut off, although it took a couple of long moments before her hand dropped from her ear.

Alexander was coming. Here. To her booth. With her artwork. Wanting to talk. He was going to set up his office and work from Strawberry Sands.

None of those things felt even remotely like reality. What in the world was she going to do?

Enjoy this preview of There I Find Love, just for you!

Chapter 1

Alexander Hudson flipped a pen through his fingers while staring out the floor-to-ceiling windows in his corner office overlooking Lake Michigan.

Chicago was his hometown, although he certainly hadn't been born on this side of it.

In fact, in order to get here, he'd had to do the opposite of everything every person who knew him expected him to do in life.

Succeed, for one.

He sighed and turned his face away from the view and walked to his desk. He picked up the water that sat there, took a swig, then walked back to the window, the pen never stopping its movement around his fingers.

Normally, Saturday mornings were his favorite morning to work. There was little noise in the offices, he was seldom bothered, the phone didn't ring much, and he and his administrative assistant, Clara, had all the time and privacy in the world to lose themselves in their work.

Except today, Clara wasn't here.

Twisting on his foot, he strode back to the desk, then turned and started back to the window without taking a drink.

She had wanted to go home.

Like Chicago wasn't her home. She belonged here. Belonged in the office with him, helping him, taking his notes and instructions, looking up information, making coffee, grabbing lunch, sending emails, and...giving a little sunshine to his soul.

He pursed his lips. Turning abruptly, he strode to the other wall, past the large windows and the beautiful view. Barely seeing it. He made a lap around his office, large and luxurious, the kind of office he could only dream about as he ascended the ladder, coming from the slums of the city one small step at a time. Through hard work, determination, and perseverance, he'd earned this corner office. And he'd worked hard to keep it.

But somehow, the success that he'd always thought would feel so good didn't really feel like success. He didn't have the satisfaction, didn't feel happy...except when he was around Clara.

She had a smile and way about her that was friendly and cheerful, even on his grumpiest days.

It was far, far different than anything he'd experienced growing up. He really didn't know anyone else like her. She trusted way too easily, which he scoffed at, warned her about, and finally had tried to protect her from. From herself.

She was so different from everyone else he knew. Most people were sarcastic and self-focused. People who would say if someone was too cheerful or too hap-py or too eager to please, they had self-esteem issues that needed to be worked on.

He'd spent enough time in therapy to know that.

But sometimes, he wondered exactly what his therapist knew. After all, from the little bit that he talked to her about personal issues, she didn't seem to have a very happy life herself.

That had made him dig deeper, and eventually he quit going. She'd been divorced twice, had been currently fighting over custody of her two children—not fighting for custody, fighting to not have it—and had been suicidal.

He considered himself a little bit crazy to be thinking that he could go to someone like that and get life advice for himself.

He wanted life advice from someone like Clara. Someone who seemed happy and cheerful, someone other people enjoyed being around and who seemed content and at peace with her life.

His entire life, he was looking for that contentment and peace. He hadn't found it yet.

That wasn't his problem this morning though.

His problem was he suspected that Clara wanted to quit.

It was something he'd heard as he was passing the water cooler the previous week. Normally, he didn't walk around without reading something. After all, there was no point in wasting any time. So normally he had his head down and didn't pay attention to the people around him. But when he heard Clara's name, his attention had been diverted. It was just a snippet of information. But the line that he'd heard, "Clara is out of here soon," had made his heart drop like a rock and his hands tremble.

There wasn't anyone else who worked in the office named Clara. Not that he knew of anyway. But just in case, he checked.

Clara Landry, his administrative assistant, was the only Clara in the company.

And apparently, she was quitting.

Just a few weeks ago, he had asked her to move to the Cities with him. He was starting a new office there, and it would take six months to a year to get things up and running. He didn't want to do it without her. Actually, he really didn't want to do much of anything without her. Funny how she'd come to be indispensable to him.

He hated that. That was why he didn't get close to people. Because they never stayed. He'd been abandoned by way too many people who were never supposed to leave him, way too many times in his life, and he should know better than to get complacent now.

The trouble was, he didn't know what to do. He could just let her go, but there was something in him that didn't want to do that.

He knew he couldn't hold her. No one could hold another person, or change them, as much as they might like to. He'd learned that with his parents.

But Clara. She was different.

He pressed his lips together as he stared out, unseeing, at the blue-on-blue beauty of Lake Michigan and the wide expanse of the sky. There had to be a way. He could offer her more money. Of course. But he'd offered her more to move to the Cities. A lot more. He already paid her more than any administrative assistant that he knew was making anywhere. It couldn't be the money.

Was it him?

People often said he was a difficult man to work for. He supposed that was true. He held others to the same high standard that he held himself to. But he didn't ask anyone to do anything that he wouldn't do himself.

Had he been unkind to her?

He supposed he'd taken advantage of her. He felt her large compensation package would keep her and hadn't considered that it might take more.

But then again, maybe what he'd overheard was just office gossip.

He liked that idea. But there was only one way to find out. He wasn't the kind of man to sit around. He pulled his phone out of his pocket and dialed Clara's personal cell phone number. It was the only number he had for her.

He tapped his fingers on his desk as he waited for her to answer.

"Hello?"

"Are you coming out to the Cities?" He probably should have tried to do some small talk, but he'd never learned how. He always cut to the chase.

"I thought I had until the middle of July to decide." Did she sound annoyed? Scared? And what was going on in the background? It sounded like she was in the middle of some kind of concert or something.

"I've changed my mind." He could hardly tell her he was scared to death of trying to do life without her in it. That she was the only bit of sunshine his soul ever saw. That she made him feel like he was almost human. He couldn't lose her, and her words sounded far too much like she was planning on telling him no and just needed more time to get enough nerve to do so.

He made a spur-of-the-moment decision. The kind of decision his gut was famous for, the kind that had landed him multimillion dollar accounts, because he wasn't afraid to lay himself out when he believed the winds were turning in his favor.

"I've decided we're both going to work remotely from that little town you want to stay in. What's it called? Strawberry Pie Place or something?"

"Strawberry Sands. It's a lakeside town." She paused, and his heart thumped hard. Was she going to say no? "You're moving here?"

He hadn't considered going quite that far. But in a snap, his mind was made up. That would work. That would absolutely work.

"Yes." He said the word with confidence. This would give her what she wanted—to live near her family—and it would give him what he wanted, too: Clara. Working for him.

His mind immediately turned the questions into answers and a to-do list. He rattled it off. "I can work remotely as long as they have good internet, and I will make sure they do. I'll have everything set up in two weeks. Send me the directions. I'll drive in today, and we'll have a meeting to hash everything out. I want the best place to set up shop. The staff you'll need to hire. Office equipment you'll need to purchase and job duties. We'll end up traveling a lot together, as we'll need to go to the Cities at least once per month for in-person meetings."

"Today?"

"Yes."

"It's Saturday."

Shoot. He'd totally forgotten. Man, she probably thought he was some kind of loser that he was in his office at this hour on a Saturday morning. Although she knew him from working with him for years and knew he worked Saturdays almost every week.

She just didn't realize what the thought of her leaving had done to him. He thought of making up some kind of excuse that he'd had a date, but she bailed, but one of the things he'd sworn he'd never do was lie. His parents had lied to him enough. He valued the truth and tried to live it. He especially wanted to do that with Clara.

"You're right. I'll buy you dinner. There is someplace to eat there, right? Then we'll talk."

"Um… I have a stand…at the…Strawberry Festival."

It was a slap in the face to be confronted with the fact that she had a life outside of his. For some reason, that made him feel left out and…lonely. That she had friends and fun and family, and he…was at his office on a Saturday morning trying to figure out how to keep his administrative assistant from quitting because she was the closest thing he had to a friend.

"Fine. We'll meet there. Text me directions."

He slid his phone off before she could turn him down. Hopefully, she would come through with directions for him. If she didn't... He picked up his phone and Googled "Strawberry Festival in Strawberry Sands." He could find her himself.

***

Pick up your copy of There I Find Love by Jessie Gussman today!

newsletter – I laughed so hard I sprayed it out all over the table!"

Claim your free
book from Jessie!